# FREE TO FIRE

Fargo had heard enough. No one paid any attention to him as he climbed down. Belinda and the farmer were arguing. He slowly drew his Colt and cocked it and fired a shot into the ground. At the blast everyone jumped and looked at him.

"What the hell?" Dogood blurted.

"Who's he?" Harold asked. "What's he doin' here?"

Fargo pointed the Colt at him. "I'm the hombre who is going to put a slug into you if you don't move."

"What?" Harold said.

"I brought the doc all this way to see your girl. She's going in whether you like it or not."

"Here now," Harold blustered. "You can't threaten a man on his own property."

Fargo cocked the Colt and at the click the farmer tensed.

"In case you haven't heard, it's a free country. I can threaten you anywhere I want."

# THE TRAILSMAN

## #363

# DEATH DEVIL

## by

## Jon Sharpe

A SIGNET BOOK

SIGNET
Published by New American Library, a division of
Penguin Group (USA) Inc., 375 Hudson Street,
New York, New York 10014, USA
Penguin Group (Canada), 90 Eglinton Avenue East, Suite 700, Toronto,
Ontario M4P 2Y3, Canada (a division of Pearson Penguin Canada Inc.)
Penguin Books Ltd., 80 Strand, London WC2R 0RL, England
Penguin Ireland, 25 St. Stephen's Green, Dublin 2,
Ireland (a division of Penguin Books Ltd.)
Penguin Group (Australia), 250 Camberwell Road, Camberwell, Victoria 3124,
Australia (a division of Pearson Australia Group Pty. Ltd.)
Penguin Books India Pvt. Ltd., 11 Community Centre, Panchsheel Park,
New Delhi - 110 017, India
Penguin Group (NZ), 67 Apollo Drive, Rosedale, Auckland 0632,
New Zealand (a division of Pearson New Zealand Ltd.)
Penguin Books (South Africa) (Pty.) Ltd., 24 Sturdee Avenue,
Rosebank, Johannesburg 2196, South Africa

Penguin Books Ltd., Registered Offices:
80 Strand, London WC2R 0RL, England

First published by Signet, an imprint of New American Library,
a division of Penguin Group (USA) Inc.

First Printing, January 2012
10   9   8   7   6   5   4   3   2   1

The first chapter of this book previously appeared in *Range War*, the three hundred
sixty-second volume in this series.

# The Trailsman

Beginnings . . . they bend the tree and they mark the man.
Skye Fargo was born when he was eighteen. Terror was his
midwife, vengeance his first cry. Killing spawned Skye
Fargo, ruthless, cold-blooded murder. Out of the acrid smoke
of gunpowder still hanging in the air, he rose, cried out a
promise never forgotten.

The Trailsman they began to call him all across the West:
searcher, scout, hunter, the man who could see where others
only looked, his skills for hire but not his soul, the man who
lived each day to the fullest, yet trailed each tomorrow. Skye
Fargo, the Trailsman, the seeker who could take the wild-
ness of a land and the wanting of a woman and make them
his own.

*1861, the Ozark Mountains—where
hate ran rampant and
life was cheap.*

# 1

Skye Fargo was deep in the Ozark Mountains. He was riding along a dirt road enjoying the warmth of the sun on his face and the light breeze that stirred the oaks and spruce when out of nowhere trouble kicked him in the teeth.

A big man, wide of shoulder and slim at the hips, Fargo wore buckskins. They were stock-in-trade for scouts, and Fargo was one of the best. Around his throat was a red bandanna, in a holster on his hip a Colt. The stock of a Henry poked from the saddle scabbard.

The Ovaro under him was often called a pinto by those who couldn't tell the difference. A splendid stallion, Fargo had ridden it for years.

Hoofprints pockmarked the dust of the road. The ruts of wagons ran deeper.

Fargo was cutting through the mountains to reach Fort McHenry. He was to report for a scouting job.

There were no Indians in the Ozarks; they had been pushed out by whites. Outlaws were few and far between. For once Fargo could relax.

That changed when the big man came to a junction and drew rein. He was sitting there watching a pair of red-tailed hawks pinwheel high in the vault of blue when the pounding of hooves and the clatter of wagon wheels drew his gaze to the south.

A black buggy came thundering around a bend, a stanhope with a closed back, the horse galloping hell-bent for leather. A woman was in the seat, staring blankly ahead, the reins slack in her hands.

Fargo caught only a glimpse of her. To him she appeared to be in shock. He reckoned the horse was a runaway and she couldn't control it. So no sooner did the buggy whip past than he reined in pursuit and used his spurs.

The Ovaro was well rested, and swift. Fargo would have caught up to the buggy quickly if not for the road's twists and bends. A straight stretch opened, and he swept past the buggy and came alongside the horse pulling it. The sorrel was lathered and straining and almost seemed to welcome the reins being grabbed and being made to come to a stop.

As soon as the buggy was still, Fargo reined around and politely asked, "Are you all right, ma'am?"

Right away two things struck him. First, the woman was uncommonly gorgeous. Her eyes were as green as grass, her lips a ruby red. She had lustrous brown hair that fell in a mane past her shoulders. Her calico dress swelled at the bosom and along her thighs.

The second thing that struck him was that she was mad as a riled hornet.

"What in God's name do you think you are doing?" she snapped.

"Saving you," Fargo said, and gave her his best smile. It had no effect.

"From what, you simpleton?"

"Hey now," Fargo said. "It looked like your horse had run away on you and—" She didn't let him get any further.

"For your information, I am perfectly fine. And Julius Caesar was doing what he's supposed to do."

"Good God," Fargo said. "Who names their horse that?"

"I have no time for this. I have no time for you. Out of my way. Your pinto is in front of my wheel."

"He's not a pinto . . ." Fargo began, and again she cut him off.

"You are a lunkhead. A handsome lunkhead, I'll grant you, but a lunkhead nonetheless. Now out of my way."

And with that she flicked her whip at the Ovaro. Fargo had no chance to deflect it or rein aside. By sheer happenstance, the snapper at the end of the whip caught the stallion dangerously near the eye, and the Ovaro did what most any horse would do under similar circumstances—startled and in pain, it reared and whinnied. In rearing, the Ovaro slammed against the sorrel, and the sorrel, too, did what most any horse would do: it nickered and bolted.

The woman cried out and tried to grab the reins but they slipped over the seat and out of her grasp.

"Son of a bitch," Fargo blurted, tucking into the saddle to keep from sliding off. The Ovaro came down on all fours and he bent and patted its neck to calm it, saying, "Easy, boy. Everything's all right."

The buggy raced around the last bend with the woman hollering, "Stop, Julius! Stop!"

Fargo had half a mind to ride on. It was her fault her horse had run off. Instead he reined after her and once again resorted to his spurs. The buggy had a good lead and the sorrel was flying. He'd catch sight of it only to have it disappear around another turn. Once he spied the woman looking back at him. She appeared to be even madder, which in itself was remarkable. Most women would be terrified. A lot of men, too.

Another bend, and the sorrel went into it much too fast.

The wheels on the right side rose a foot and a half off the ground. For several harrowing seconds Fargo thought the buggy was going to go over but the wheels crashed down again. The buggy commenced to sway wildly, the rear slewing back and forth. He heard the woman bawl for Julius to stop. He got the impression that the sorrel was, in fact, slowing, when the tail end of the buggy whipped more violently than ever and it went over.

The woman screamed.

Oblivious, the sorrel galloped another forty feet, dragging the buggy after it, until Fargo again came alongside and brought the animal to a standstill. Reining around, he vaulted off the stallion. He was worried he'd find the woman with her neck broken or her ribs staved in but she was alive and well and clinging for dear life.

"Here," Fargo said, offering his hand. "Are you all right, ma'am?"

The woman looked around in bewilderment and then at him and her daze was replaced by anger. Letting go, she heaved out of the buggy, pushing his hand away as she stood. "No thanks to you, you dumb bastard," she fumed. "You nearly got me killed."

"You're the one who hit my horse," Fargo reminded her. "That was a damn stupid thing to do."

"So now this is my fault?" she said, gesturing at the buggy.

"If the petticoat fits," Fargo said.

She smoothed her dress and snapped, "I don't think I care for you very much, Mr.—?"

Fargo told her his name, along with, "And I don't give a damn what you think." He stepped to the buggy. "But I'll do what I can to get you on your way, Miss . . . ?"

3

"It's doctor to you," she said resentfully. "Dr. Belinda Jackson."

"You're a sawbones?" Fargo could count the number of times he'd run into a lady sawbones on one hand and have four fingers left over.

"Why not? Because I'm a woman I'm not fit to be one?"

"I never said any such thing," Fargo replied.

"But I bet you were thinking it," Belinda said. "All you men are alike. You think only men can be physicians. My own father tried to talk me out of going to medical school. And the instructors, all men, treated me as if I had enrolled on a lark and wasn't to be taken seriously. Now here I am, with my own practice, and I'm being treated the same way by the very people I took the Hippocratic oath to treat." She had grown red in the face during her tirade. "It's not fair, I tell you."

"Life has a way of doing that," Fargo said as he slowly moved around the buggy, inspecting it for damage.

"Well, aren't you the buckskin philosopher?" Belinda said. "Any other insights you care to share?"

"Only that you're not going anywhere," Fargo said, and pointed at the wheel the buggy lay on. Several of the spokes were shattered. "I was going to find a pole and see about getting you on your way, but without a wheel there's not much point."

"Oh no." Belinda came over and sank to her knees. "Can't we fix it somehow?"

"I don't usually carry spokes in my saddlebags," Fargo remarked.

"A philosopher and a humorist," Belinda said. "Do you cook as well?"

"Lady," Fargo said, "I'm a scout."

"I was only joking." Belinda stood and moved around to the other side and groped under the seat. "I guess you'll have to take me. I can't afford more delays."

"Take you where?"

"To the McWhertle farm. Their youngest girl is sick. They sent word over an hour ago. I was on my way there when you spooked my horse."

"I'm not the one with the whip," Fargo said.

"There you go again." Belinda stopped groping and pulled a black bag out. "Ah. Here it is. We'll have to ride double and I expect you to behave yourself."

**4**

"I haven't said I'll take you."

Belinda walked up to him. Most of the color had faded from her face but her eyes were flashing. "Listen to me. Their girl is ten years old. From what they told me it sounds serious. I have to reach her as quickly as possible."

"That's why you were driving your buggy so fast," Fargo realized.

Belinda moved to the Ovaro and held her arms aloft. "Are you going to be a gentleman or must I climb on by myself?"

"What about your horse?" Fargo proposed. "I'll strip off the harness and you can ride it."

"Bareback?" Belinda waggled her arms. "I don't ride well, I'm afraid. If I could, do you think I'd be using a buggy? No, we'll leave it here and I'll retrieve it on my way back to Ketchum Falls."

"That a town?" Fargo asked. If it was, he'd never heard of it.

"A settlement, more like." Belinda waggled her arms some more. "Do I have to light a fire under you? If you were any slower you'd be a turtle. Time's a-wasting."

Fargo sighed. He set the black bag down, swung her up, and gave the bag to her. Carefully forking leather so as not to bump her with his leg, he suggested, "Wrap your arm around my waist so you don't fall off."

"Your shoulder will do nicely."

"Suit yourself." Fargo clucked to the Ovaro and felt her fingers dig deeper. "Keep on north, I take it?"

"For a couple of miles yet, yes. We'll come to an orchard and there will be a lane on the right."

Fargo figured she wouldn't say much, as mad as she was. She surprised him.

"I suppose I should apologize for treating you so poorly. But I'm worried about Abigail. That's the McWhertle girl's name. She's a pretty little thing."

"You're a pretty thing, yourself."

"Why, Mr. Fargo. Was that a suggestive remark?"

"If suggestive means I think you'd look nice naked, then yes," Fargo said.

For the first time since he'd met her, Dr. Belinda Jackson laughed. "My word. You don't beat around the bush, do you?"

Fargo thought of the junction of her thighs, and grinned to himself. "I like to get right to things."

5

"Is that so?"

Before Fargo could answer, a man came out of the woods at the side of the road. The man was wearing a bandanna over the lower half of his face and holding a rifle that he trained on Fargo's chest.

"That's far enough!" he commanded. "I'll have your money or I'll have your life."

# 2

Fargo drew rein. He could tell by the voice that the would-be robber was young. His right hand was on his hip close to his Colt, and he was uncommonly quick at drawing it. But instead of drawing he gave the fool a way out by saying, "You don't want to do this, boy."

"The hell I don't," the young man said, his words muffled by the bandanna.

"I don't have much in my poke," Fargo said. "It's not worth dying over."

The young man motioned with the rifle. "You're the one who will die if you don't quit yappin' and hand it over."

Dr. Belinda Jackson astonished Fargo by poking her face past his shoulder and saying, "Timothy Wilson, you stop this nonsense this minute—you hear me?"

The young man's eyes widened and he lowered the rifle a little. "Dr. Jackson? I didn't see you up there behind that feller."

"Of course you didn't," Belinda said. "You don't have your spectacles on."

"What the hell?" Fargo said. "You know this jackass?"

"I couldn't find them this mornin'," Timmy said to her, letting the rifle dip to his waist. "But I don't need 'em to hit the center of a blob." He coughed a few times, and sniffled.

"A blob?" Fargo said.

"He doesn't see very well," Belinda said. "Astigmatism, it's called. People to him are shapeless blobs."

"So I just aim at the middle," Timmy said in a tone that suggested he thought it was awful smart of him. He did more coughing.

"How many people have you shot?" Fargo wanted to know.

"None yet," Timmy said, sounding disappointed that he hadn't. "But give me a few years and I reckon I'll have done in as many as Dastardly Jack."

7

"Who?"

Timmy came closer. "Don't tell me you never heard of him? Why, he's the most famous highwayman in Merry Olde England. Ain't that right, Doc?"

"According to the stories," Belinda said. "You might want to take your bandanna off. It's sticking to your mouth when you talk."

"Oh. Sure." Timmy pulled the bandanna down around his throat. His nose was running and he wiped it with a sleeve. To Fargo he said, "You're not pullin' my leg, mister? You've never heard of the Prince of Highwaymen? I got me two of his adventures. I can read, with Ma's help. I have to stick my face right up to the page, but they are the best books ever."

"Books?" Fargo said.

"Penny dreadfuls," Belinda said. "From England. His mother bought them for him at the general store a few months ago, and ever since, he's gone around pretending to rob folks."

"Pretending?" Fargo said.

Timmy looked mad. "I ain't neither. I'm doin' it for real but no one will take me serious. Everyone in these parts knows me so when I try to rob them they tell me to shush and behave and go on their way."

"But you keep trying?"

Timmy nodded. "I want to be just like Dastardly Jack. Have all that money. Wear fine clothes. And them ladies swoonin' at my feet. Just like in the pictures in those books." He brightened and declared, "I thought for sure I'd get money from you, you bein' a stranger and all."

"What if I'd shot you, you dumb bastard?"

"Why would you do that?"

Fargo stared at him. "Some people, boy, don't like being robbed."

"Well, that's just petty." Timmy coughed and grumbled, "This damn cold."

Belinda said, "I've told you before, Timmy. Those stories are fiction. They're make-believe."

"How can that be, Doc?" Timmy said. "They're writ down, ain't they?"

To Fargo the doctor said, "He thinks that anything on a printed page is real."

"I need a drink," Fargo said.

"I got me some squeezin's," Timmy said. He slid a hand under his shirt and produced an old battered flask. Smiling, he came over and handed it up. "My pa makes it himself in a shed out back of the barn. Ma won't let him make it in the barn on account of the smell."

Fargo uncapped the flask, wiped it on his buckskins, and took a swig. He'd had moonshine before and was braced for the jolt. Or so he thought. His throat seared with liquid fire and a keg of black powder went off in his gut. It was so potent, it set his eyes to watering and his nose to running. Coughing and hacking, he wiped at his face with his sleeve.

Timmy cackled. "Has a kick, don't it? My pa likes to say that if liquor don't curl a man's toes, it ain't worth drinkin'."

"Good stuff," Fargo wheezed, and gave back the flask.

"Any time you want a swig, just say so," Timmy said, sliding it under his shirt.

"You're the strangest damn outlaw I ever met."

"Hey now," Timmy said. "No need to be insultin'. I ain't no outlaw. I'm a highwayman. Or I will be once I can get folks to give up their money."

"Why don't you go home, Timmy?" Belinda said. "I have to get to the McWhertle's. Abigail is sick."

"So is Old Man Sawyer, I hear," Timmy said. He coughed some more. "I'm comin' down with somethin', too." He sighed and cradled his rifle. "Oh well. Guess I'll rob me somebody another time." He grinned and walked off into the woods and coughed and wiped his nose and cheerily waved.

"That boy is going to get his fool head blown off," Fargo predicted.

"We should pay Old Man Sawyer a visit after we're done with Abigail McWhertle," Belinda said.

"We?"

"You keep forgetting that thanks to you I don't have any means of getting around."

"I should have gone the long way around these mountains," Fargo said.

"Sorry?"

"Nothing." Fargo gigged the Ovaro.

"Don't take this personally," Belinda said, "but you're a little strange."

"I'd fit right in around here."

"I don't see what you mean by that. The people in these parts are as normal as anywhere. Most are farmers or have small homesteads and grow vegetables and raise hogs and the like. And as for Ketchum Falls, it's no different from any other settlement. Most of the folks there are earnest and hardworking. No one is strange."

"Tell that to Dastardly Timmy."

"Oh, posh," Belinda said. "His only problem is that he's young yet, and doesn't know his own mind."

"If he has one."

"Now you're being mean. It's perfectly normal for a boy his age to have a hero they look up to. Why, when Timmy was younger, his idol was Robin Hood. For the longest while he ran around with a bow and arrows and called all the women maiden-this and maiden-that. He was adorable."

Fargo grunted. "Did Robin Tim shoot anyone with those arrows of his?"

"Well, there was an incident," Belinda said, and laughed. "But it was mostly comical."

"Mostly?"

"Mr. Barnaby, the banker, is the wealthiest man hereabouts. He has a fine house over on Turner Creek. One day Timmy snuck up on him and threatened to put an arrow into him if Mr. Barnaby didn't turn over all his money."

"That's sure comical," Fargo said.

"But the money wasn't for Timmy. He wanted it to give to the poor, exactly like Robin Hood did. You know. Rob from the rich and give to the poor? Everyone thought it was precious of him, despite the calf."

"There's a calf in this now?"

"Mr. Barnaby thought the whole thing was a great joke. He laughed and told Timmy he wouldn't give him any money and to run along. So Timmy let fly with an arrow."

"I knew it," Fargo said.

"Unfortunately, Timmy wasn't wearing his spectacles and he missed by a mile. Or at least thirty feet. The arrow hit a calf over in the corral. Pierced its eye, if you can believe it, and the poor thing dropped dead then and there."

"Arrows in the eye will do that."

"Well, it was an accident, plain and simple. No one held it against Timmy."

"Not even Barnaby?"

"He was upset, certainly. But Timmy's father made it right by offering to pay for the calf in installments. I'd imagine it's paid off by now."

"You know that boy will shoot someone with that rifle. It's only a matter of time."

"We don't know any such thing. Timmy will grow out of his highwayman phase sooner or later and no real harm will have been done. Boys will be boys, after all."

"How old is he, anyway?"

"Eighteen."

Fargo snorted.

"What?"

"Nothing," Fargo said.

"You say that a lot. But go ahead. Mock us all you like. We're proud of our community. It's not much by big city standards but Ketchum Falls is a nice place to call home."

"Unless you're a calf."

"Now you're being silly."

After that they rode in silence until they came to half an acre of apple trees and a rutted dirt track.

"That's the orchard and the lane," Dr. Jackson said, pointing.

"Must be all of ten apple trees," Fargo remarked.

"What's your point?"

The lane wound through the trees and past a field of corn to a two-story stone farmhouse. Beyond was a barn and an outhouse. Parked in front of the house was a van with a two-horse team.

Fargo felt Belinda's fingers dig into his arm and her face poked past his shoulder.

"God Almighty. Not *him*. If Harry McWhertle sent for that scoundrel, so help me, I'll pin his ears back."

"Who are you talking about?" Fargo asked in mild confusion.

Belinda jabbed a finger at the van. "Can't you read?"

The van had been painted a bright yellow except for the seat, which was pink. On the near side, in black block letters, was the glowing pronouncement: CHARLES T. DOGOOD, MASTER OF PATENT MEDICINES. NOSTRUMS FOR ALL AILMENTS. REASONABLE RATES.

In smaller letters was the claim: CURES FOR GOUT, LIVER DISEASE, KIDNEY DISORDERS, CONSTIPATION, HEADACHES, TOOTHACHES,

11

FEMALE COMPLAINTS, INCONTINENCE, HEART PAINS, LUNG DIS-
ORDERS, TOE FUNGUS, EARWAX BUILDUP, DRY SKIN, DANDRUFF,
NAIL-BITING, AND SUNDRY NERVOUS CONDITIONS. SATISFACTION
GUARANTEED OR HALF YOUR MONEY REFUNDED.

"Is there anything he doesn't cure?" Fargo said, but Belinda
didn't answer. She slid off and started for the porch, muttering to
herself.

The screen door opened and out strode a tall man in a knee-
length coat that had seen better days and a straw hat frayed around
the edges. His face made Fargo think of a ferret, only ferrets were
better looking.

Belinda Jackson stopped and shook a fist at him.

"Dogood! How dare you. I have half a mind to take a scalpel
and slit your throat."

The patent medicine man balled his fists. "I'd like to see
you try."

# 3

To Fargo it appeared that Dr. Jackson might charge up the steps and tear into Charles T. Dogood but just then the screen door opened again and out came a stout middle-aged woman wearing an apron and with her hair in a bun. She had a kindly face, at the moment etched by sorrow.

"Dr. Jackson!" she exclaimed in relief. "You've come at last."

"My buggy overturned, Edna," Belinda said, hurrying to the woman's side and glaring at the patent medicine salesman as she went past him. "Has there been any change in Abigail?"

The woman sadly shook her head.

"I must see her immediately," Belinda said.

The screen door creaked a third time and a man as stout as Edna emerged. He had small eyes and his chin was covered with stubble. He didn't look happy to see the physician. "What's this? What's she doing here?"

"I sent for her, Harold," Edna said.

"I told you we don't need her," Harold said. "We have Dr. Dogood."

The patent medicine man puffed out his chest and sneered at Jackson.

"He's not a doctor," Belinda said heatedly. "He sells quack concoctions, for God's sake. *I'm* the real doctor. We've been all through this before, Harold." She went to go by but he stayed in the doorway. "Let me through."

"I told Edna plain," Harold said. "You weren't to come. Dr. Dogood has been treatin' the folks hereabouts for goin' on twenty years. You've been here how long? Four? Five?"

"What does that have to do with anything?" Belinda demanded.

"I don't trust you and your newfangled doctorin'," Harold said. "I heard tell that the time you treated the Clovis boy, he died."

13

"He ate some rat poison. He was too far gone by the time they sent for me. There was nothing I could do."

"Sounds like an excuse to me." Harold folded his arms and shook his head. "No, ma'am. You ain't gettin' inside and that's final."

"Oh, Harold," Edna said.

"You shush, woman," Harold told her.

Charles T. Dogood smiled and nodded. "You're doing the right thing, Harold. The bottle I've sold you will cure your little girl in no time. I stake my reputation on it, and as you know, I am held in the highest esteem by everyone for miles around."

"Please let me in," Belinda pleaded. "I'm the only real hope your daughter has."

"Go back to Ketchum Falls. You're not wanted here."

Fargo had heard enough. No one paid any attention to him as he climbed down. He stretched, then stepped to the bottom of the steps. Belinda and the farmer were arguing. He slowly drew his Colt and cocked it and fired a shot into the ground. At the blast everyone jumped and looked at him.

"What the hell?" Dogood blurted.

"Who's he?" Harold asked. "What's he doin' here?"

Fargo pointed the Colt at him. "I'm the hombre who is going to put a slug into you if you don't move."

"What?" Harold said.

"I brought the doc all this way to see your girl. She's going in whether you like it or not."

"Here now," Harold blustered. "You can't threaten a man on his own property."

Fargo cocked the Colt and at the click the farmer tensed.

"In case you haven't heard, it's a free country. I can threaten you anywhere I want."

"What a preposterous thing to say," Dogood said. "Have you no common sense, my good fellow?"

"Take your hat and throw it into the air," Fargo commanded, and motioned at the sky.

"My hat?" Dogood said in confusion. "What on earth for? I'll do no such thing."

Fargo leveled the Colt at him. "Either you will or I will."

Dogood's Adam's apple bobbled. "I don't see—" he said. But

he removed the straw hat and stepped to the edge of the porch and threw it high.

Fargo fired and the hat danced in midair. He fired again and it flipped and fell with a fluttering motion to land in a flower bed. He twirled the Colt several times, then cocked it and pointed it at Harold. "You were saying?"

Harold stared at the six-shooter, his jaw muscles working. Finally he swore and moved from the doorway.

Belinda darted inside, Edna hastening after her.

"I'm obliged," Fargo said to the farmer. He spun the Colt into his holster.

"I'm goin' in, too," Harold said, and turned to do so.

"No," Fargo said. "You're not."

"I don't know who you think you are," Harold fumed. "I'm warnin' you now, if you don't stop this, this instant, I'm goin' to sic the law on you."

"And I'll be your witness," Dogood said. "My honesty is considered impeccable."

Fargo jabbed a thumb at the van. "All those cures you brag about. Do you have a cure for being stupid?"

"You are plumb ridiculous," Harold said. "No one has a cure for that."

"Too bad," Fargo said.

The patent medicine man's ferret features twisted in resentment. "You're implying that Harold and I are in need of such a cure, am I correct?"

"He's what, now?" the farmer said.

"How about the two of you come down here and sit on the steps and we'll talk about cows and such?" Fargo said. He took a few steps back, his hand on the Colt.

The two men glanced at one another, and obeyed. Dogood glowered. Harold McWhertle muttered and clenched and unclenched his hands.

"The marshal will put you behind bars for this. Just see if he doesn't."

"How many cows do you have?" Fargo asked.

"Twenty-seven. Prime milk cows, every one. Why do you want to know?"

"How would you like to have twenty-six?"

"You're threatenin' my *cows*?"

"I could use a beefsteak," Fargo said.

"He's playing with us, Harold," Dogood said. "He thinks we're a couple of country hicks."

"He does?"

Dogood sniffed at Fargo and declared, "I'll have you know, sir, that I am regarded far and wide as an excellent authority on ailments of all kinds. As my good friend Harold, here, mentioned, for more than twenty years, more than two whole decades, I've roamed the highways and byways of this wonderful county offering my humble services to those in need."

"That he has," Harold confirmed with a bob of his chin. "Charles T. Dogood is a saint."

"How much do you charge?" Fargo asked.

Dogood's nose wrinkled in irritation. "I must make a living, the same as everyone else. That I charge for my nostrums is no different from your physician friend charging for her pokings and proddings."

"You tell him, Dr. Dogood," Harold said.

"A dollar a bottle? Five dollars a bottle? Ten dollars a bottle?" Fargo said.

"I am on to you, sir," Dogood said. "You're suggesting that I fleece my customers. Were I less compassionate, I'd take umbrage at your calumny."

"He only charged us two dollars for the swamp root and celery," Harold came to Dogood's defense.

"Swamp root and what?" Fargo said.

Dogood smiled. "Remarkably efficacious for the cure of fever, and sweet young Abigail is burning up."

"Are there any swamps hereabouts?" Fargo asked.

"You don't give up, do you?" Dogood said. "For your information, I have many of the ingredients for my nostrum *remediums* sent to me from far and exotic lands, the better to treat the afflicted."

"He's a marvelous man," Harold said.

"My swamp root comes from the deep, dank swamps of Louisiana," Dogood went on. "It is sent to me in powdered form by a local lad who scours the swamps near his home for the roots I require. Once every few months, without fail, Sir William—that's what I affectionately call the young gentleman—sends me a new shipment. If you don't believe me you can ask the Ketchum Falls postmaster."

"I recollect you tellin' me about him," Harold remarked.

"Yes, sir," Dogood said. "Swamp root. Eel skin. The eyes of newts. The extract from hippopotami gall bladders. I could go on and on. The entire world is my pharmacopoeia. I spare no expense in the interests of healing."

"I told you he was wonderful," Harold said.

"You don't happen to have a bottle of whiskey lying around, do you?" Fargo asked.

"No. Why?"

Fargo sighed.

"I am on to you, sir," Dogood said. "And I must say, you are uncommonly intelligent for one of the buckskin-clad brigade. Or is it that you are naturally cynical?"

"Naturally what?" Harold said.

"Don't let his appearance deceive you, Harold," Dogood said. "This man is as shrewd as they come."

"I thought he was uppity," Harold said.

"Of course you did. I've often said, and you can ask anyone, Harold, that you are a man of discernment. No one pulls the wool over your eyes."

"That they don't," Harold agreed.

"Are you sure you don't have a bottle?" Fargo asked again.

Hooves drummed on the lane and two riders came out of the orchard at a trot. One was huge and wore overalls and a floppy hat. The other was rail thin.

"Why, look who it is," Dogood said. "Providence has intervened in your behalf, Harold."

The farmer's face mirrored delight. "Now we'll see who tells who what, by God."

Fargo didn't like the sound of that. He hooked his thumbs in his gun belt and shifted to one side so he could watch the approaching riders and keep an eye on McWhertle and Dogood.

"If I were you, mister," Harold said, "I'd climb on that pinto and light a shuck."

"And quickly," Dogood encouraged him.

"I'll leave when the doc does."

The riders were almost there. The huge one had a moon face, a sloping forehead, and beetling brows. The thin rail had a nose that hooked like a bird's beak and a chin that curled up at the end. They came to a stop in puffs of dust and the huge man leaned on his saddle horn.

"Howdy, cousin Harold. I came to borrow those shears we talked about last Sunday at church."

"Cousin Orville," Harold replied. "Cousin Artemis," he said to the skinny one. "Am I glad to see you two." He gestured at Fargo. "This gent, here, pulled his gun on me."

Orville sat up. "He did what, now, cousin?"

"My Abigail is sick and my wife sent for that female sawbones. I forbade her to step foot in my house but this feller skinned his smoke wagon and made me step aside."

"Did he, now?" Orville dismounted and strode up to Fargo, towering a good foot and a half over him. "Mister, you just bought yourself a heap of trouble."

# 4

Artemis had alighted, too. He sidled to the left with a hand behind his back.

"I'd be obliged if you'd make him scat," Harold said to Orville.

"What is kin for?" Orville rumbled, and poked Fargo in the chest with a finger as thick as a railroad spike. "You heard him, mister. You got two choices. Skedaddle, or be pounded to a pulp."

"You call that a choice?" Fargo said, and hit him. He slammed a solid uppercut to the jaw that would have toppled most men or at least set them back on their heels but all Orville did was sway and grin.

"Not bad. I ain't been hit that hard in a coon's age. But I have a jaw like an anvil."

"Hell," Fargo said.

"My turn," Orville said, and swung.

Fargo ducked, slammed a fist into the farmer's ribs, and winced. It was like hitting metal bars. Sidestepping, he dodged a jab, slipped in close, and let fly with three quick punches to Orville's gut. All Orville did was grunt.

"Pound on him fierce, cousin!" Harold hollered. "He has it comin'!"

Orville raised both fists and waded in.

Fargo retreated. He couldn't match the man, brute strength against brute strength, but he was quicker with his hands and on his feet. He hoped to avoid the other's blows long enough to tire him.

"Fight, consarn you," Orville said.

Fargo skipped away to gain space to move.

"You are commencin' to annoy me."

"Want me to help?" Artemis offered. "I'll hold him while you beat on him."

"It's mine to do," Orville said without taking his eyes off Fargo.

Fargo thought about resorting to the Colt but as near as he could tell the farmer wasn't armed. Iron-hard knuckles clipped his shoulder and spun him half around. Once more he backpedaled.

"You've got him on the run, cousin!" Harold whooped. "Give him what for."

Lumbering in, Orville did something Fargo didn't expect—he kicked him. The boot caught Fargo in the thigh and he stumbled and tripped and fell on his back.

"Finish him!" Harold squealed.

Orville grinned and spread his hands. "I'm about to bust you good, mister."

Not if Fargo had anything to do with it. He lashed out with his right foot. He was going for Orville's knee but kicked Orville's shin, instead. Orville grimaced and halted and glanced down.

"That hurt."

"Careful cousin," Artemis cried.

The porch was at Fargo's back. Suddenly whirling, he jumped, caught hold of the rail, and swung up and over.

"Look out, Dogood!" Harold shouted, and rose from the steps and backed away, apparently in the belief that Fargo might attack them.

"Never let it be said that Charles T. Dogood was cowed by an uncouth ruffian," the patent medicine man declared. "Be my witnesses, friends, that I laugh in the face of danger." And he uttered a bark of mirth.

Fargo would have liked to shoot the whole damn bunch.

Orville lumbered up the steps. He had to duck his head under the overhang. Then, standing so Fargo couldn't get past him, he said, "Are you a man or a chipmunk?"

"Chipmunk?" Harold said. "Ain't it supposed to be a mouse?"

"In my esteemed opinion he's more like a jackrabbit," Dogood interjected. "It's a wonder he doesn't possess long ears and a bobbed tail."

Orville said, "Well, whatever he is, I've got him now." He advanced with his arms spread wide.

Fargo couldn't get around him without being grabbed. He didn't bother to try. Instead, he whirled, placed both hands on the rail, and vaulted over it. He landed in the exact spot he had been standing a minute ago.

"Damn it to hell," Orville exclaimed. "I can't thrash him if I can't get my hands on him."

"Leave it to me, cousin," Artemis said, and his hand came from behind his back holding a knife. Grinning, he moved it in small circles. "Stand right where you are, mister, if you know what's good for you."

Fargo glanced past him and feigned shock. "Will you look at that. There's a cow trying to climb an apple tree."

"No foolin'?" the skinny farmer said, and looked over his shoulder.

Fargo kicked him in the groin.

Artemis dropped the knife and clutched himself and doubled over, his face turning cherry red. "No fair," he gurgled, and tottered.

"What do you call two on one?" Fargo rejoined, and laid him out with a right and a left cross. He stood over him, ready to swing again, but Artemis was out to the world. Before he could congratulate himself, a vise clamped on to his left arm and he was spun roughly around.

"I've got you now, you blamed frog," Orville said.

Fargo punched and kicked and sought to wrench free. Orville absorbed the punishment without flinching and gripped him by the other hand, and smiled.

"This is goin' to hurt, mister."

Fargo rammed his knee at Orville's privates. It had worked for Artemis but didn't work now. Orville moved and took the brunt on his tree trunk of a leg, and then he grinned and in an incredible display of raw might, he swung Fargo over his head and held him there, saying, "This is how I bust those who rile me."

Fargo kicked and pushed but he was helpless. He attempted to twist so his back took the impact but he wasn't half around when he smashed into the ground so hard, he'd swear that every rib in his chest shattered. Flooded with agony, he nonetheless tried to rise.

"You're a tough one," Orville complimented him. "I'll have to bust you twice." He reached down to lay hold and do it again.

Fargo had one chance. He marshaled all his strength, and rolled. Orville missed. Scrambling backward, Fargo dug his left hand into the ground. When Orville scowled and lunged, he threw a handful of dirt into the farmer's eyes.

"Damn it all," Orville cried, and stopped and swiped at his face. "He's trickier than a fox."

"I'll help you," Harold said, and started to move around behind Fargo.

By then Fargo had the Colt out and the hammer back. "Like hell you will."

Harold froze.

Dogood took a step and Fargo swung the Colt to cover him. "I'll shoot the next son of a bitch who moves."

"He shows his true colors, my friends," the patent medicine man declared.

Orville was blinking his eyes. Both were watering and his cheeks were stained brown. "You'd shoot me even though I ain't armed, mister?"

"Try me," Fargo said. With difficulty he pushed to his knees and from there to his feet. His body hurt all over.

"I should of known," Orville said.

"All of you sit on the porch," Fargo directed.

"And if we don't?" Harold challenged.

"You'll spend the rest of your days walking around without a knee," Fargo said.

"We could rush him, all of us at once," Harold said. "He can't get all of us."

"I'm not much of a fighter, I'm afraid," Dogood said. "The most I can offer is moral support." He was the first to sit. Draping his arms over his legs, he said, "It won't hurt to rest here a spell and hear what the doctor has to say about sweet little Abigail."

Harold reluctantly sank down. Artemis was still unconscious on the ground.

That left the big man. Orville squinted at Fargo and at the Colt and said, "This ain't over. Me and you have a score to settle."

Fargo pointed the Colt at Orville's left leg.

"But it won't be right this minute," Orville said. "You have the upper hand. We'll meet again, though. Count on it. And next time things will be different."

"Sit," Fargo said.

"I don't think I like you," Orville said, but he finally sat.

Fargo breathed an inward sigh of relief. His left side was throbbing and it was all he could do to stand up straight.

"What I want to know," Harold said, "is what the lady doc is doin' up there?"

"Probably taking Abigail's pulse and using her stethoscope," Dogood said. "And after a while she'll prescribe a medicine that is no more effective than any of mine, and likely less so."

"Damn doctors, anyhow," Harold said.

"Why are you so against them?" Fargo asked.

"Mainly I'm against the female ones. Women ain't got no business doin' man's work."

"Who says only men can be doctors?"

"Why, most everybody hereabouts," Harold said. "It's like bein' a lawman or an undertaker. Some jobs ain't fit for females."

"Amen to that," Orville said. "I was over to the county seat last month and there was a woman clerk at the bank."

"You've got to be joshin'," Harold said.

"As God is my witness," Orville said.

"Women ain't got a head for numbers. What were they thinkin', hirin' her?"

"She was a right pretty filly," Orville said. "I reckon that had somethin' to do with it." He wiped at his running eyes and then stabbed a finger at Fargo. "How about you, mister? I take it you reckon female sawbones are fine."

"Female anything is fine by me," Fargo said.

"God Almighty," Harold said. "Next thing you know, this jasper will say it's all right to give women the right to vote."

Dogood laughed.

"I don't know about that one," Orville said. "My wife would like to and I can't say as I blame her."

"Cousin Orville!" Harold said in dismay.

"Well, it don't take much brains to savvy politics," Orville said. "You just naturally figure all of them are liars and vote for the one who lies the least."

"Them there are wise words," Harold said.

The door opened and out came Belinda, appearing downcast. Behind her was Edna.

"How did it go?" Fargo asked.

"Abigail has a fever of a hundred and one," Belinda informed him. "I can't account for it just yet, but she shows some symptoms that worry me. I haven't ever seen them before. I need to consult my medical books."

"You see?" Dogood said to the men. "Incompetence is the natural result of allowing a woman to do a man's work."

"For two bits I would shoot you," Belinda told him.

"Hell," Fargo said. "For two bits I'll shoot all four of them."

No one was amused.

# 5

They were almost to the end of the lane when Belinda mentioned, "You said you would take me to visit Old Man Sawyer, remember?"

Fargo mentally vowed to never again chase a runaway buggy. He didn't care how good-looking the driver was. "How far is it?"

"Only a couple of miles farther," she answered. "He lives at the end of the road."

"It figures."

"I'm sorry to impose."

"You almost sound like you mean it," Fargo said as he reined to the right.

"I do."

She had softened some toward him, and Fargo liked that. He found himself dwelling on her physical charms and daydreaming about how nice it would be to see her without clothes on.

Around them the countryside teemed with life. In the apple trees sparrows flitted. A robin was having a tug of war with a worm. Several deer were grazing. A monarch butterfly flew past, its wings fluttering.

Fargo breathed deep of the many scents, and winced.

Belinda was craning her head past his shoulder and noticed. "Are you all right? When I came out I saw that you appear to have been in a scuffle."

"You could call it that."

"Where does it hurt?"

Fargo told her about his left side.

"I'd best have a look at you," Belinda said, and pointed at a shaded nook under several maples. "Pull up there and I'll examine you."

About to say she didn't need to bother, Fargo imagined her fingers on his body, and grinned. "Whatever you say, Doc."

"I wish all men had your attitude."

Fargo drew rein, gave her a hand down, and dismounted. He pried at his buckskin shirt and got it high on his chest. "Will this do?"

She set her black bag down. "That will do fine." With experienced care she ran her hands over his ribs, pressing here and there and asking, "Does this hurt?" or "Does that hurt?"

One bruise, in particular, caused Fargo to grit his teeth and hiss like a kicked snake.

"I suspect your rib is fractured," Belinda said. "I can wrap you when we get to my office although it will heal on its own provided you don't get into any more scuffles."

"Around here there's no telling," Fargo said.

Belinda did more poking. She didn't find anywhere that hurt as much but she pointed out a few bruises. "You took quite a beating, didn't you? What caused it, anyhow?"

Fargo told her.

"Ah. Then it's my fault. I know how they feel about women doctors."

"Or females in any line of work."

"Yes," Belinda said. She grinned. "I sometimes marvel that they stoop to having sex."

Fargo chuckled and paid for it with more pain. Grimacing, he said, "I wouldn't mind stooping with you."

"Need I remind you I'm a doctor?"

"Last I heard, only nuns take vows of chastity." Fargo had met one not long ago so he should know.

Belinda laughed but caught herself. "That's not the point. I must be professional. I can't let my personal feelings influence me."

"You're saying you have feelings for me?"

"I most certainly do not." Belinda picked up her bag. "Let's be on our way, shall we? I'd like to make it back to Ketchum Falls by nightfall."

They passed several more farms and homesteads. At one place a dog came to the edge of the road and barked furiously. At another, several small children waved and smiled.

"I do so love it here," Belinda said, her breath warm on his ear.

"It has its charms," Fargo said, thinking of her breasts against his back.

The road narrowed. The tracks and ruts became fewer. Eventually it petered out at the border of dense woodland. A trail led deeper in.

"That will take us to Old Man Sawyer's," Belinda said. "It's not much farther."

Fargo kneed the stallion. Shadows dappled them as the trees formed a canopy overhead. He listened for the usual sounds but didn't hear so much as a bird. "That's peculiar."

"What is?"

"It's too quiet."

"Oh. You're right. I hadn't noticed."

Fargo grew uneasy. It was unnatural, the silence. He placed his hand on his Colt.

They went around a bend.

Ahead, the trail ended at a clearing. In the center stood a small cabin.

"Good God," Belinda blurted.

Fargo drew rein and palmed the Colt, his skin prickling. He'd seen worse sights but nothing like this.

Dead animals were scattered everywhere. Most were chickens, either with their necks twisted or their heads wrenched off. At a corner of the cabin lay a hog. Its belly had been sliced from end to end and its intestines had oozed out in coils. Farther back was a mule. Its throat had been cut and it lay in a scarlet pool, long since dry.

"Why, that's every last animal Old Man Sawyer owns," Belinda said breathlessly. "Who could have done this?"

Fargo was wondering the same thing. "Stay on the Ovaro," he said, and swung down. He hadn't taken more than a couple of steps when her elbow brushed his. "Damn it. Why didn't you listen?"

"I have to see if Old Man Sawyer is alive."

"I can do that for you."

"I'm not climbing back on. Let's proceed, shall we?"

"Stay behind me." Fargo came to the first chicken. Around it in the dust were the tracks of the culprit. "What kind of footwear does Old Man Sawyer wear?"

"Boots, as I recall," Belinda said. "An old pair, all scuffed and cracked. Why?"

Fargo didn't answer.

The cabin door was open. It was dark as pitch inside, and in the darkness, something moved.

Fargo stopped and cocked the Colt. "Come out with your hands where I can see them!" he shouted.

"Do you see someone?"

"I saw something. I don't know what it was."

A dog staggered out of the cabin, an old hound with more wrinkles than Methuselah.

"Oh no," Belinda said.

The dog was coated with blood. One of its ears had been cut off and its body bore multiple punctures from a knife or some other sharp tool. It looked at them and whined and collapsed.

Belinda tried to go past Fargo but he held her back.

"That's Old Man Sawyer's dog, Rufus. The old man loved it as if it was his son."

"Stay back," Fargo insisted. He went ahead, never taking his eyes off the dark rectangle of the doorway. Sinking to a knee next to the hound dog, he touched it and it licked him.

"Who could have done that?" Belinda hadn't listened—again— and had come up.

The old hound whimpered.

Fargo stared at the chickens and the hog and the mule. If he had been in Arizona or New Mexico he might suspect Apaches.

"We better go in and see if Sawyer is there," Belinda said, and tried to go past him.

"Not we," Fargo said. "Me. And this time, damn it, do as I say."

"I don't like being bossed around."

"How do you feel about being dead?" Fargo nodded at the carnage. "Whoever did this might be inside."

"Oh." Belinda put a hand to her throat. "I hadn't thought of that."

"Stay the hell put."

Fargo warily moved closer. If he had to guess, he'd say the slaughter had been done early that morning. He skirted a last chicken. The cabin was quiet. Sidling to the jamb, he poked his head in. It smelled, but no worse than most cabins where the occupants hadn't washed in a month of Sundays. "Sawyer? You in here?"

There was no reply.

Fargo moved along the outer wall to the window. Instead of glass it was covered by burlap. He pushed the burlap aside and a splash of light bathed the interior. The place was a shambles. A table had been overturned. A chair had been splintered. The contents of the cupboard had been cast about.

A shirt had been ripped to pieces.

"Will you look at that," Belinda said at his shoulder.

Fargo swore.

"What's the matter?"

"You don't listen worth a damn." Fargo let go of the burlap and returned to the hound. It was breathing in ragged gasps, its sides heaving.

"The poor thing isn't long for this world," Belinda said. "There's nothing I can do."

"I can put it out of its misery," Fargo said, and thumbed back the hammer.

"No. Please. Let the poor thing die on its own."

Fargo took aim at its head.

"How can you be so heartless?" Belinda demanded.

"You want it to suffer?" To Fargo's way of thinking, that was more heartless.

"No, I don't. But if I went around killing everyone who was suffering, I'd never heal anyone."

"That's not the same. There's nothing you can do for him. You said so, yourself."

"I know. But it seems so cruel."

Fargo took aim again but lowered the revolver. While they'd been arguing the hound had died. "Damn."

"We still have to find out who did this."

"Maybe it was Dastardly Timmy."

"Don't even joke about a thing like that. Timmy is a sweet boy deep down."

"Except when he's pointing rifles at people and killing calves with arrows."

"You're a cynical man—do you know that? It's a wonder you can trust anyone."

"I trust me," Fargo said.

In the woods a twig snapped.

Fargo spun and crouched. Someone, or something, was out there. Twigs didn't break on their own.

"What was that?" Belinda asked.

Realizing she was still standing, Fargo grabbed her wrist and yanked her down beside him. "Do us both a favor and try to stay alive."

"What do you think I have been doing?"

"Being an idiot."

"That was rude. If you're going to insult me all the time—" Belinda didn't finish.

Off in the woods someone laughed. Not a normal laugh but a titter that grew louder and rose higher in pitch the longer it went on. From the titter it swelled to a cackle that almost seemed inhuman. The cackle rose to a shriek and the shriek to a scream. Suddenly it faded to a titter again. The titter, in turn, dwindled to silence.

"What in heaven's name?" Belinda blurted.

Fargo's sentiments exactly.

# 6

Fargo had a decision to make. Go after the screamer or stay with the physician. "I'm getting you back to the settlement," he informed her.

"But the man in the woods—"

"Is loco or drunk," Fargo said. He gestured at the dead animals. "And if he did that, think of what he might try to do to us."

"You're worried about me," Belinda said. "If I wasn't here you'd try to find him."

"Maybe not," Fargo hedged. "I fight shy of lunatics."

"I won't be mollycoddled," Belinda said, shaking her head, and before he could divine her intention or stop her, she was on her feet and moving toward the forest.

"Damn it. Hold on," Fargo said, but she didn't stop. He rose and caught up and grabbed her by the arm. "What in hell do you think you're doing?"

"I already told you," Belinda said, trying to pull free. "We have to see who that is."

"Like hell." Fargo hauled her toward the horses but she dug in her heels. Fuming at her stubbornness, he was about to bend and throw her over his shoulder when an arrow arced out of the trees and flashed between them, missing his face and hers by no more than a few inches.

"Oh my," Belinda exclaimed.

Fargo spun and banged two swift shots at the undergrowth in the direction the arrow had come from. Hoping that would buy them the time they needed, he wrapped his left arm around her waist, swept her off her feet, and propelled her bodily toward the Ovaro.

"What are you doing?"

"Saving you whether you want to be saved or not." Fargo fired again. They reached the stallion and he pushed her at it and barked,

"Climb on." For once she listened. He was about to fork leather when he spied a dark silhouette amid the trees. Another arrow flashed, nearly clipping his hat. He thumbed the hammer and squeezed the trigger and the figure vanished. He doubted he'd hit whoever it was.

The next instant Fargo was in the saddle and reining away from the cabin and the slaughtered animals. He glanced back but the figure didn't reappear. At the trail he brought the Ovaro to a trot and held it until they reached the road. From there he went at a gallop and didn't slow until he'd put half a mile in their wake.

"That was something," Belinda said when she could talk without having to shout.

"We were lucky," Fargo said, and commenced to reload.

"There haven't been Indians in these parts for ten years or more."

"That was no Indian," Fargo said. "It was a white man."

"How do you know?"

"He missed."

"Oh, please," Belinda said. "Some Indians are terrible shots with a bow just as some whites are terrible shots with a rifle."

Fargo had done enough arguing for one day. He was content to stay quiet, but she wasn't.

"We'll have to notify Marshal Gruel although I don't know what good that will do. The good marshal doesn't take his job seriously enough."

"Oh?" Fargo said.

"It's not that he's incompetent," she elaborated. "Far from it. When he sets his mind to something, he does it well. The trick is to spur him to action."

"Is that your way of saying he's lazy?"

"If he were any lazier he would have moss growing between his toes." Belinda sighed. "You don't mind, do you, if I rest my cheek on your shoulder? All this activity has left me a bit peaked."

"Rest away," Fargo said. He felt her lean into him, felt the swell of her breasts on his back. She had a nice body, this lady doc.

"First Abigail and now this," Belinda said. "It's been a day to remember."

And it wasn't over yet, Fargo almost said. He looked back a few times but no one was shadowing them. Eventually they passed the McWhertle orchard and farm and not long after that they reached her buggy. He climbed down and unhitched her horse. Since she couldn't or wouldn't ride bareback, he threw his rope over it and led it back.

Belinda told him her life story. How she was born and raised in New Jersey. How her mother died after a long illness. Consumption, it was. While watching the family physician tend her, and seeing how kind and sympathetic he was, Belinda first entertained the idea to take up medicine. Her father, who owned a market, eventually came around to the idea of his daughter becoming a doctor and encouraged her to pursue her dream, and after years of hard study she earned her degree.

"It wasn't easy," she concluded. "And I don't mean just the schooling. I was the only woman in my class, and I was ruthlessly teased."

"Isn't ruthless a little strong?"

"One time they stuck a cadaver in my bed. Another time they hid my instruments so I would miss important surgical practice. They constantly needled me. And when I bore it in good stride and didn't report them, guess what? Did they accept me? No. It made them angry." Belinda paused. "I'll never forget the night four of them cornered me behind the lecture hall and groped me and stripped me naked and then sent me on my way with a smack on my fanny. And do you know what?"

"No. What?"

"When I finally went to the dean, they were given a three-day suspension. That was their punishment. They deserved a lot worse."

"What brought you to Arkansas?"

"Opportunity. Ketchum Falls advertised for a physician. I answered and they accepted, and I've been fighting for acceptance ever since."

"It'll come."

"I'm afraid my faith in human nature isn't what it once was," Belinda said. "I no longer care if it comes or not. I do this for me, not for them."

"Them" turned out to be the three hundred and twenty-seven people who called Ketchum Falls home. The settlement got its name from a small creek with a ten-foot waterfall that fed into a shallow pool.

In the heat of the afternoon the streets were quiet. Most everyone was indoors. A dog sprawled in the shade of a water trough raised its head to watch them go by. A pig with piglets grunted.

Belinda asked Fargo to take her to the livery. It was at the far end of the main street. They were climbing down when a heavy man carrying a pitchfork came out and grunted much as the pig had done.

"Doc," he said simply.

"Mr. Simpson, I've had a mishap."

"A what, ma'am?"

"An accident. My buggy has overturned and a wheel is broken. I'd like for you to fix it."

"No, ma'am," Simpson said.

"But you're also the town blacksmith, are you not? And I understand you've fixed wagons for others."

"That I have but I won't fix yours."

Fargo had been listening with half an ear but now he turned. "Let's hear your reason."

"I don't need to give one," Simpson said. "This is my business and I can do as I damn well please."

"Not you, too, Mr. Simpson?" Belinda said. "I thought you accept me for what I am."

"I tolerate you, ma'am," Simpson said. "And only because my missus makes me." He smirked. "And you forget, ma'am. Orville and them are kin and he and Artemis were by here earlier."

"So that's it," Belinda said. "But I need my buggy. I can't make house calls without it. How about if I pay you twice the going rate?"

"Head over to the county seat," Simpson suggested. "Could be you can find someone to repair that wheel."

Belinda was crestfallen. "Why, it's a day and a half there and back. And how am I to get there without my buggy?"

"I'll rent you a horse."

Fargo had reached his limit. "I have a better idea," he said. "Gather up your tools and be ready in fifteen minutes and I'll be back to take you to her buggy."

Simpson tilted his head. "Mister, if I won't fix it for her, what in hell makes you think I'll fix it for you?"

"Your teeth," Fargo said.

"What about them?"

"Either you fix her buggy or you gum your food from here on out."

"Was that a threat?"

"It sure as hell was."

Simpson held the pitchfork so the tines were pointed at Fargo's chest. "I'll give you one minute to vacate these premises."

"Remember, I'll be back in a quarter of an hour," Fargo said. Wheeling, he strode out and led the Ovaro to a hitch rail and looped the reins.

Belinda came up behind him. "What did you hope to accomplish, bluffing like that?"

"Who said it was a bluff?" Fargo leaned against the hitch rail. He could use a drink but he needed a clear head.

"You can't threaten people like that."

"Don't your ears work?"

"Yes, I heard you perfectly fine. And Mr. Simpson certainly took you seriously. I had to plead with him not to report you to Marshal Gruel."

"I don't have a watch so I'd guess he has about thirteen minutes left."

"You can't just march in there and kick his teeth in."

"I'd use this," Fargo said, and patted the Colt.

"What manner of man are you? As much as I need my buggy, you can't flaunt the law."

"Twelve minutes," Fargo said.

"Listen to reason, will you? Besides, he'll be waiting for you and he'll have that pitchfork."

"Pitchforks don't shoot very far."

Belinda tiredly rubbed the back of her neck. "Will you be serious for five seconds? I'm starting to like you and I'd hate to see you behind bars."

"You are, are you?" Fargo grinned and winked. "How about the two of us go out for supper later? My treat."

"You're an exasperating man—do you know that?"

"I hear that a lot," Fargo said. "And we're coming up on ten minutes."

Belinda put her hand on his arm. "Stop this silliness," she said softly. "I won't have you getting hurt on my account. If you truly want to help, escort me to the county seat at Wickerville."

"Won't need to," Fargo said.

Setting her black bag down, Belinda faced him and placed her hands on his chest. "What will it take to bring you to your senses?"

"A kiss would be a good start," Fargo said.

Belinda touched her lips to his chin.

"I said a kiss, not a chicken peck." Fargo straightened and started to walk around her but she held on to his wrist.

"I refuse to let you do it."

"You can't stop me."

"No," Belinda said, and she smiled and nodded down the street. "But he can."

A man wearing a badge was coming toward them.

# 7

The lawman was almost as wide as he was tall and he wasn't much over five feet. He wore baggy clothes that lent the illusion he was a walking tent. A faded brown vest twice the size it should be added to the illusion. A floppy hat crowned his head. He didn't wear a revolver; he carried a sawed-off shotgun. And he was carrying it by holding it by the twin barrels. "How do you do, Doc?" he greeted her, his speech as slow as a turtle's walk.

"I'm fine, Marshal Gruel," Belinda replied. "What brings you out in the midday heat?"

"Your friend, here," Gruel said in his slow way, and studied Fargo with mild interest. "A complaint has been filed against you, mister."

"By whom?" Belinda asked.

"Orville McWhertle. He says your friend attacked him and did bodily harm."

"That's a lie. Orville started it."

"You saw the fight with your own eyes, Doc?" Gruel asked without taking his eyes off Fargo.

"Well, no," Belinda admitted.

"Then how do you know who started it?"

"Because Skye wouldn't."

"Skye, is it?" Marshal Gruel said, his thick lips curling slightly.

"Now don't you start, Seymour," Belinda said.

"Seymour?" Fargo said.

"My ma's doin', bless her empty head," Gruel said. "And you have no room to talk, *Skye*."

"You can't arrest him," Belinda said.

"I'm afraid I have to. Orville has witnesses who are willin' to swear in court that your friend attacked him without cause."

"Let me guess. Artemis and Harold."

"And Dr. Dogood," Marshal Gruel said. "His sworn deposition

will carry a lot of weight. No one in our community is more respected." To Fargo he said, "I hope you'll come along peaceable."

"No," Fargo said.

Marshal Gruel blinked. "How's that again? You're not goin' to come along nice and quiet-like?"

"I'm not letting you arrest me today."

"Are you loco?" Marshal Gruel said as if he wasn't sure he had heard right.

"I'd be stuck in your jail for how long?" Fargo said. "Days? Weeks? Longer? Then you'll take me before a judge who happens to be a third cousin to Orville McWhertle and he'll sentence me to sixty days or a fine of a thousand dollars or however much it will be, and either I pay or you'll have me scrubbing floors and cleaning your outhouse every day until my sentence is up."

"Are you implyin' the law in Ketchum Falls is crooked?" Marshal Gruel asked.

"Does bear shit stink?"

The lawman scratched the stubble on his double chin. "Well, now. This makes for a quandary, don't it?"

"Quandary?" Belinda said.

"I can't know big words?" Gruel did more scratching. "Tell me, mister. What do you aim to do if I try to do my duty?"

"Stop you."

"Are we talkin' fists or a knife or lead or what?"

"Let's put it this way," Fargo said. "It's good there's a sawbones handy."

"I can't believe you would disobey a minion of the law like this," Belinda said. "You're only getting yourself into worse trouble."

"I can believe it," Marshal Gruel said.

"You can?"

Gruel nodded. "A man does what I do, he has to be good at readin' folks." Gruel slid his hand from the shotgun's twin barrels to the front end of the forestock. "Orville McWhertle is as big as a tree with more muscles than an ox. Any gent who will stand up to him has to be as tough as they come or stupid. The moment I set eyes on your friend, here, I knew he wasn't short on brains."

"That's very perceptive of you, Marshal," Belinda said.

"Meanin' I'm smarter than you thought?" Gruel grinned. "That's all right, ma'am. A lot of folks make the mistake of thinkin' that all

I have between my ears is empty space." Gruel eased his fingers from the front of the forestock to the middle.

"I never suggested you were stupid, Seymour."

"It would please me considerable if you'd stop callin' me that," Gruel said. "Anyway"—he smiled at Fargo—"I reckon you and me are at what they call an impasse." His hand was almost to the back end of the forestock.

"Don't," Fargo said.

"Don't what?" Gruel said, but his hand froze.

Fargo placed his hand on his Colt. "Don't try to use that scattergun."

The lawman smiled and switched his hand to the barrels. "You don't miss much, do you?" He gazed at the buildings on the right side of the street and at those on the left. At a number of windows faces peered out. Most were women and children. "It's temptin' to see if you're really as tough as I think you are but it wouldn't do for us to gun each other down with all these folks lookin' on." He half turned. "You've got me over a barrel this time, mister. Next time, I won't make the mistake of bein' polite."

"Leave it be," Fargo said.

Gruel tapped his badge. "Can't. Mind you, I'm not takin' sides, neither. Orville has a temper, so it wouldn't surprise me a lick if he was the one started things. But a complaint is a complaint and I have to act." He started to walk off.

"Wait," Belinda said. "You haven't heard about Old Man Sawyer, have you?"

"What about that old coot?"

Belinda gave an account of the slaughtered animals and the strange scream. "We never did see sign of him," she finished up. "He might be lyin' off in the woods somewhere, scalped."

"If it ain't chickens, it's feathers," Gruel said. "I'll let the sheriff know."

"Isn't it your job to go see?"

"I'm the marshal, Doc. My jurisdiction is Ketchum Falls. Anything outside the town limits is county jurisdiction, and Old Man Sawyer lives as far out as you can go. It's a job for county law. That would be Sheriff Baker." Gruel touched his hat brim to her, stared hard at Fargo, and waddled off down the dusty street.

"I don't think he likes you very much," Belinda commented.

"The ten minutes are up," Fargo said, and strode toward the livery.

"Wait." Belinda hustled to overtake him. "Will you do me a favor? Will you not get into an altercation with Mr. Simpson?"

"That depends on Simpson."

As they neared the livery a buckboard rattled from behind it with the liveryman in the seat. Tied to the back of the buckboard was the physician's horse. Simpson came to a stop next to them and patted the seat. "I've got my tools in the back. You can ride with me if you'd like, ma'am."

"Why the change of heart?" Belinda asked.

Simpson glared at Fargo.

"Oh. Yes. Well, in any event, I'm grateful." Belinda clambered up.

"I'll follow you," Fargo said. "And I'm obliged, too."

Simpson scowled. "To her I'll be nice but you can go to hell, gun hand." He flicked the reins and the buckboard clattered on.

Fargo retraced his steps and climbed on the Ovaro. On the way out of town he passed the marshal's office. Gruel was at the window and watched him go, scowling.

The day was hot. Fargo wanted a drink and was hungry as hell. A couple of times he started to doze and shook his head to stay awake.

Halfway there, they encountered the patent medicine man coming from the other direction in his van. Charles T. Dogood smiled and waved to Simpson and the doctor. But as he went past the Ovaro he scowled.

"It's a regular epidemic," Fargo said.

With his help it took the liveryman no time to right the buggy but half an hour to replace the broken spokes. As soon as he was done, Simpson climbed on his wagon, wheeled it around, and headed back.

Fargo mentally bet himself that he'd get another scowl.

He won the bet, and sighed.

"Something the matter?" Belinda asked.

"I don't recollect ever meeting friendlier folks anywhere," Fargo said.

"I can get back on my own. But I do want to thank you for all your help." Belinda offered her hand and he shook it. "I'm hoping you'll let me repay you by coming to my house for supper tonight instead of us going out to eat."

Fargo let his gaze roam from the swell of her bosom to her long legs. "I never say no to a free feed."

"Good." Belinda told him how to find her place, climbed in, and picked up the whip. She went to flick it, and paused. "You'll be careful, won't you? You've made a few enemies today, I'm afraid."

"I'm collecting them," Fargo said.

"I can't help but feel it's mostly my fault."

"You can't cure jackasses."

"They're not bad people," she said. "They're close-minded, is all."

"You can make excuses for them all you want," Fargo said, "but a son of a bitch is a son of a bitch."

"You *are* a hard one," Belinda said.

Fargo thought of what he would like to do with her after supper. "You haven't seen hard yet," he said with a straight face. He stood there while she wheeled her buggy toward the settlement. Once she was out of sight he climbed on the Ovaro. Instead of reining after her, he rode in the opposite direction.

"I've never been fond of folks trying to kill me," he said to the stallion. "An eye for an eye, I always say."

The sun was high in the sky when he reached the clearing in the woods. A legion of flies swarmed the dead animals. The cabin door was partway open. He saw no movement within.

Fargo alighted and palmed the Colt. Holding the reins in his left hand, he stalked into the woods near the point where the bowman had let the arrows fly. The ground was covered with leaves and pine needles that didn't bear tracks well. He found a few scuff marks, enough to tell him that the archer wore boots and not moccasins.

The scuff marks led deeper in.

Climbing on the Ovaro, Fargo tracked his quarry. Or tried to. After only fifty feet the marks ended. He rode in circles seeking to find sign again, and couldn't. Drawing rein, he said quietly, "It's one of those days."

The Ovaro pricked its ears.

From out of the undergrowth came a maniacal shriek, part laugh, part scream. It was so close that Fargo gave a start and jerked the Colt up. He glimpsed a figure and went to shoot but the figure melted away. A jab of his spurs and he rode toward it.

Another shriek, from the left, warned him the figure had changed position.

Fargo shifted in the saddle.

There was the distinct *twang* of a bowstring and an arrow streaked out of the foliage toward his chest.

# 8

Luck favored Fargo. The arrow clipped a tree limb and was deflected instead of burying itself in his flesh.

Fargo fired at the vegetation where the arrow had come from and jabbed his spurs. He skirted several trees. Up ahead, a dark figure was bounding like an antelope. He fired again and the figure cackled and disappeared.

"Not this time," Fargo said. He reached the spot and scoured the woodland. Whoever the man was—and Fargo had his suspicions—he was a damn ghost.

A thicket crackled. Fargo caught sight of a flying form. He sought to overtake it but there were so many trees and boulders, he couldn't gain.

A pair of spruce reared in front of him. Fargo plunged between them, their branches so thick, it was a wonder he didn't lose an eye. He burst into the clear—and hauled on the reins.

A steep bluff fell before him, a drop of sixty or seventy feet. In a slew of dirt he slid the Ovaro to a stop and gazed down at jagged boulders.

Fargo's skin crawled at how close he had come. He was sure the man had deliberately lured him there to send him over the edge. Another maniacal laugh caused him to rein around and resume the chase. The figure bounded and leaped with the agility of a jackrabbit. He saw flying white hair and what might be a brown coat.

"Hold on there!" Fargo hollered, but he was wasting his breath. Once again the figure vanished.

Fargo had the feeling he was being played for a fool. The man he was after knew the woods well. He must be careful not to be tricked a second time.

Another screech keened, the demented cry of an earthbound banshee.

Fargo reined toward the sound and rose in the stirrups, hoping for another glimpse of his quarry. The undergrowth thwarted him; it was too heavy.

Acting on inspiration, Fargo drew rein. If he couldn't catch the bastard, maybe he could lure him out. Cocking the Colt, he held it close to his hip, ready to shoot. A somber quiet fell.

Fargo felt unseen eyes on him. Tensed to dive from the saddle if another arrow was let fly, he waited. The seconds dragged into minutes but nothing happened.

A bush thirty feet away moved.

Fargo pretended not to notice. Out of the corner of his eye he saw the stems part. There was the suggestion of a face.

The tip of an arrow slowly aligned with his body.

Fargo swiveled and fired twice, fanning the hammer. At the second blast the man bleated and rose and fled. Fargo saw white hair but not the man's face. Eagerly, he came to a gallop.

The fleeing form darted around a pine. Seconds later Fargo did the same. Too late, Fargo saw an oak tree—and a low limb.

He tried to rein aside but the limb caught him across the chest and slammed him out of the saddle. The pain was excruciating. He was dimly aware of flying and hitting so hard, the world spun. His world blinked to black for a few seconds; then his senses returned in a rush. He sat up. The blow hadn't done his ribs any favors. His side hurt worse than ever. He realized he had dropped the Colt and groped for it, and then a shadow fell across him.

An old man stood a few yards away. In his left hand was a bow, at his hip an empty quiver. His white hair and age-ravaged face were bespattered with dry scarlet drops from the animals he had killed. His bloodshot eyes glittered like quartz. The man laughed his crazy laugh, exposing yellow teeth.

"Sawyer?" Fargo said.

The man dropped the bow.

"I'm a friend of Doc Jackson's," Fargo said. "Why the hell are you trying to kill me?"

Sawyer—if that was who it was—tittered and danced a little jig.

"Answer me, you damned lunatic."

Suddenly the man went into violent convulsions, his arms and legs jerking spasmodically. Simultaneously, a white froth oozed from his mouth.

"What the hell?" Fargo blurted.

**43**

The foam continued to spill out, dribbling down the man's chin and over the front of his shirt.

"What in hell's the matter with you?"

The convulsions stopped. The man stood still. He stared blankly at the sky and at the trees and at Fargo. He gurgled, and reached under his coat.

"Hell," Fargo said.

The old man drew a knife.

Fargo spotted his Colt. He pushed up and lunged but the man sprang in front of him. Cold steel sought his jugular. He rolled and came up in a crouch and the old man laughed and came at him again. There was a sharp prick on his shoulder.

Falling back, Fargo kicked him in the leg.

The white-haired loon howled and stumbled but he recovered in a twinkling.

Fargo dived for the Colt. His fingers touched the grips but he had to roll away to avoid another thrust of the man's knife blade.

The old man cackled and hopped up and down.

Pushing to a knee, Fargo slid his fingers into his boot. "Let's see how you like it," he growled in fury, and drew the Arkansas toothpick. As it came clear the old man did the last thing Fargo expected—he whirled and ran.

Fargo scooped up his Colt, took several bounds, and stopped in disbelief.

The man was gone.

Fargo searched everywhere; behind trees, behind boulders, behind a log.

Nothing.

Fargo's fury climbed. He'd been made a fool of—again. Climbing on the Ovaro, he expanded his search. For half an hour he scoured the forest and finally had to admit defeat. It was as if the old man had vanished into thin air.

Fargo headed for the cabin. He didn't know what to make of his clash. He'd heard tell that people foamed at the mouth when they had rabies, and he wondered if the old man had been bit by a rabid animal and come down with the disease. He'd have to ask Belinda Jackson about the symptoms.

Flies were still crawling all over the carcasses. Half a dozen buzzards had also arrived and were tearing at the mule, save for one of the big birds that was partial to pig meat. Flapping noisily when he came out of the woods, they rose into the sky and circled.

Fargo reined up and slid down. Yanking the Henry from the scabbard, he worked the lever to feed a cartridge into the chamber. Striding to the door, he kicked it and entered. Every article Old Man Sawyer owned had been broken, shattered, or torn. Clothes and blankets were in tatters. A wooden spoon and wooden fork had been snapped in half. A hatchet had been buried in the wall and left there.

Fargo tried to recall if he'd ever heard tell of rabies victims going berserk and destroying their personal effects.

Venturing back out, he made a circuit of the cabin. The stench of death was becoming abominable.

A bold buzzard about to alight took wing, hissing like a struck rattler.

Fargo didn't find what he was looking for: a dead coon or some other wild animal that may prove it was rabies.

A glance at the sun told him he had barely enough time to reach the settlement for his supper date with Belinda. Climbing on the Ovaro, he rode to the trail and was starting up it when crazy mirth erupted from the depths of the shadowed woods.

The old man was mocking him.

Fargo didn't stop. At the road he brought the Ovaro to a trot. He was so engrossed in trying to make sense of it all that when he neared the apple orchard, he didn't pay much attention to the lane that led up to the McWhertle farm. If he had, he might have noticed the two riders.

The pair gigged their mounts to the middle of the road and stopped.

"Hold it right there!" Orville bellowed.

"Just what I need," Fargo said as he drew rein.

"We saw you go past earlier and waited," Artemis informed him. "We knew you'd be comin' back this way." He said it as if it were a brilliant deduction, and beamed.

Fargo deflated him by saying, "Can you count to twenty without taking your shoes off?"

"Enough of that," Orville McWhertle snapped. "Where's your lady friend?"

"Safe from you," Fargo said.

Orville jabbed a finger at him. "You listen, mister, and you listen good. You've got no call buttin' in to our affairs like you done. There's a lot of us who don't want that lady doc around."

"So I gathered."

"Then gather this," Orville said. "If I want to, I can round up enough men to run you out of Coogan County."

"It would be interesting to see you try."

"I ain't scared of you," Orville boasted. "You got the better of me once but it won't happen a second time."

Fargo placed his hands on his saddle horn. "Are you scared of rabies?"

Orville and Artemis swapped puzzled expressions and the latter said, "Are you callin' us mad dogs?"

"I take it you haven't heard about Old Man Sawyer," Fargo said, and jerked his thumb in the direction he had come from. "I've just come from his place."

"What about him?" Orville asked.

"All his animals are dead. Everything in his cabin is in a shambles. And he's running around cackling at everybody." Fargo didn't mention that the old man was shooting arrows at everybody, too.

"You're makin' that up," Artemis said.

"What reason would I have?" Fargo retorted. "I went out there to try and find him for the doc but he's a crafty bastard. It wouldn't surprise me if he starts biting people soon."

"You're serious, by God." Artemis looked worriedly at his huge cousin. "Rabid folks do that, you know. They go around bitin' people and makin' others rabid, too."

"Why warn us when we're out to bust your skull?" Orville asked suspiciously.

"I don't give a damn about either of you," Fargo confessed. "It's the families around here I'm thinking of."

"Damnation," Artemis said. "We've got to find Charlie Dogood. I bet he has a cure for rabies like he does most everything else."

"First we check this buckskin bastard's story," Orville said. "We'll ride out to Sawyer's right this minute and have a look for ourselves."

"Be my guest," Fargo said, and reined aside.

The pair went past in a hurry.

Fargo smiled and waved and said under his breath, "Some days I scare myself." Whistling, he continued on and reached Ketchum

Falls as the sun was relinquishing the vault of sky to budding stars. He had no trouble following Belinda's directions to her house. It was one of the nicer ones, with a picket fence and a flower garden. He dismounted at the gate, tied the reins, and went up a path to the porch. The door had an oval pane of glass, and when he knocked, he saw her bustle down the hall with an apron around her waist. She had put on a fancy dress and done up her hair.

"You came," she said cheerfully as she opened the door.

"Did you think I wouldn't?"

"I'm not the best cook in the world," Belinda said, taking his arm and ushering him in. "There might be nothing worth eating."

Fargo stared at the junction of her thighs. "I bet there will be," he said.

# 9

Belinda Jackson needn't have worried. She was a damn good cook.

Their meal began with soup, an Italian soup, of all things, with a lot of noodles and a zesty sauce. Fargo had two bowls. The main course consisted of roast beef with thick gravy, potatoes, peas, and carrots. There was fresh-baked bread and salad. Fargo carved off a slab of beef that would choke a black bear and drowned it in gravy. He heaped so much butter on his potatoes, they dripped yellow drops. His peas and carrots he mixed together and sprinkled enough salt on them to make it look like snow. As for the bread, he cut each slice half an inch thick and smeared it with more butter.

"So you like my food, then?" Belinda asked halfway through the meal.

"I am in hog heaven," Fargo said with his mouth full, and smiled. He wasn't one of those who thought the way to a man's heart was through his stomach. The way to his heart was by a woman lifting her skirts. But it was a close thing.

"Save room for dessert."

"Don't you worry." When it came to food, Fargo was the first to admit he was a bottomless pit. Part of it was he spent so much time deep in the wilds that fine meals like this were few and far between. When an occasion came along, he made the most of it.

"You sure do love to eat," Belinda observed.

"I love other things too," Fargo said, and gazed at her breasts. If she noticed she didn't let on.

For dessert she gave him a choice: a slice of cherry pie or a slice of apple pie. He couldn't decide so he had a slice of both.

"My word," Belinda said. "Where do you store it all? I doubt there's an ounce of flab anywhere on that fine body of yours."

"There's not," Fargo took pride in saying. He grinned. "Been noticing that, have you?"

Belinda's cheeks turned pink. "Purely in a professional capacity, I assure you. Physicians do that."

"I do something similar," Fargo said.

"How's that?" she asked.

"I undress women with my eyes."

Her pink cheeks became red. "I've noticed. You're quite brazen about it. How about in real life? Have you undressed a lot of ladies like me?"

"One or two," Fargo said. "A lot of them undress themselves."

"You're awful cocksure of yourself," Belinda remarked, and realizing what she had said, her entire face became a beet. "Oh my. I didn't mean that the way it came out."

Fargo laughed. "That's all right." He looked her in the eyes. "Maybe I can show you before the night is out."

Belinda coughed and changed the subject.

After the meal they repaired to the parlor. Belinda bid him sit on the settee and she brought a tray with a pot of coffee and a china bowl with sugar and another with cream.

Fargo had three cups while he listened to her talk about her childhood and doctoring and how difficult it was for a female doctor to be taken seriously and for females in a man's world to make a go of it.

"You're lucky you were born a man," she commented. "There are days when I wish I'd been."

"I'm glad you're not," Fargo said.

She blushed again. "I'm serious. It's been so hard to gain acceptance here. Maybe a third of the community doesn't mind that I'm a woman. Another third doesn't much care one way or the other. The rest, especially the Mr. McWhertles, wouldn't let me treat them if they were at death's door."

"So don't treat them and let them die."

"That's harsh."

"They want to be that dumb, let them."

"There's more to it than that," Belinda said. "I have a thorn in my side, a gadfly who whispers slander in their ears and they believe him."

"Charles T. Dogood," Fargo guessed.

Belinda nodded. "He's a quack. What he doesn't know about medicine would fill the Grand Canyon. But that doesn't stop him from selling his so-called cures. I had a couple of them analyzed by a chemist friend. Dogood's cure for what he calls night fits is eighty percent alcohol."

"Pretty smart on his part."

"How can you say that?"

"Get someone drunk enough and they'll pass out. No more night fit."

Belinda looked surprised. "I hadn't thought of that but you're right. So naturally anyone who takes that thinks it works." She paused. "But some of his nostrums do more harm than good. His cure for female complaints has opium in it."

"I bet a woman feels right fine after taking a spoonful," Fargo said.

"That's not the point. Opium is addicting. Take enough and you can't ever stop."

"So he has a steady supply of customers."

"I hadn't thought of that, either. I just figured he threw in any old ingredients. But perhaps there's more to his methods than I suspected."

"He doesn't strike me as dumb."

Belinda frowned. "Why do you keep complimenting him? He's my mortal enemy, for God's sake."

"It's good to know how an enemy is."

Belinda didn't seem to hear him and went on. "If not for Dogood, a lot more people would have accepted me by now. I've tried and tried to make them see that he's nothing but a charlatan but they swear by his cures."

"If I was drinking eighty-proof alcohol, I'd swear by his cures too."

"You're not the least bit funny."

"Seems to me you need to relax a little more," Fargo suggested.

"Relax how?" Belinda said without thinking. "I'm too overwrought half the time."

Fargo set his cup on the low table by the settee and slid across until their legs brushed. "I know a way."

"Oh," Belinda said.

Fargo reached up and lightly ran a hand through her hair. She smiled nervously and placed her hand on his leg and then took it off and closed her eyes. "Something the matter?" he asked.

Belinda nodded.

"Am I supposed to guess or will you tell me?"

"I sensed . . ." she began, and swallowed. "I sensed that you were . . . how shall I put this? Interested in me?"

"That's as good a way as any."

Belinda opened her eyes and bit her lower lip. "I'm not very experienced at this sort of thing."

"You must see naked people all the time," Fargo joked to put her at ease.

"It's not the same." She bowed her head. "Oh God. I'm behaving like a child. But I've only ever been with one man in my life. We were engaged to be married. He left me when . . ." She stopped.

"We don't have to talk about it," Fargo said. He'd rather not talk at all.

"No. It's all right." Belinda gazed at the window. "He courted me for three years. We agreed that we would wait to marry until after I was done with medical school. But it was hard, I guess, my being so busy with my studies that I hardly had time for him. One day, clear out of the blue, he stunned me by saying he couldn't go on with the way things were. Either I devoted myself to him or he would leave me. He actually gave me an ultimatum. Be a doctor or be his wife."

"You chose the doc."

"What else could I do?" Belinda said, and her eyes moistened. "By then I'd invested too much time, to say nothing of money, in my education. I couldn't up and quit. I tried to make him see that. I told him that as soon as school was over, I was his. But he said that once I became a doctor, I'd be working all hours of the day and hardly ever around, and he didn't want a wife who was never home." She sighed. "And do you know what? He was right. I haven't been with a man since."

Fargo remembered a comment Harold McWhertle made to the effect that she arrived in Ketchum Falls three or four years ago. "That's a long time to be alone."

Belinda nodded, and swallowed. "Now you understand why I'm a bit apprehensive."

"Have any liquor in the house?"

Belinda chuckled. "What, you think if I'm drunk, I'll relax and enjoy it more?"

"Might work," Fargo said. He was pleasantly surprised when she nodded and stood.

"Do you know what? I'll by God do it. It's been too long since I let down my hair."

"Or your dress," Fargo said.

Belinda laughed and sashayed out, saying over her shoulder, "I have a bottle of Monongahela in the kitchen. I'll be right back."

Fargo stretched his arms along the settee. A good meal, some whiskey, and a fine figure of a woman. Life didn't get any better than this. He patted his stomach and heard the clink of glasses and she came around the corner smiling.

"Here we go."

The bottle, Fargo noted with satisfaction, was three-fourths full.

Belinda set the glasses on the table, opened the bottle, and poured barely enough whiskey to fill a thimble into each glass.

"Is that all the coffin varnish you can handle?" Fargo said. "I like mine to the brim."

"Sorry. I'm used to always staying sober in case my services are called on in an emergency."

"There's no emergency now."

From outside came the drum of hooves. A horse whinnied, and someone yelled, and in a few moments her front door shook to hard pounding.

"Dr. Jackson?" a woman hollered. "Are you in there? We need your help!"

"Who can that be?" Belinda said in alarm, hurrying from the parlor.

Fargo went with her.

The pounding grew frantic.

Belinda called out that she was coming. She opened the door and exclaimed, "Edna McWhertle! What on earth is wrong?"

The farmer's wife clasped her hands in appeal. "It's our cousin, Artemis. You have to come quick."

"Hold on," Belinda said. "Earlier today your husband practically threw me off your farm. Now you want me to come back out there?"

In a rush Edna said, "Harold's not there now. He went off with the others. And Artemis needs help bad. Dogood can't do anything. He's not a surgeon."

"Try to stay calm and start from the beginning. What exactly ails your cousin? And where did your husband go off to?"

"I'm sorry," Edna apologized. "It's just that Artemis isn't long for this world, I fear. He was shot with an arrow."

"An arrow?" Belinda said, and glanced at Fargo.

Fargo pretended to look shocked. "How could that have happened?"

"You don't know?" Edna said. "Orville told us it was you who sent him and Artemis out to Old Man Sawyer's place. Somethin' to do with rabies. That's where Artemis took the arrow in the back."

"All right," Belinda said. "You can tell us the rest on the way. I'll fetch my bag."

"We'll be out at the gate," Edna said, and hastened down the steps. Out by the fence were two lathered horses, another woman on one of them.

Belinda shut the door and looked at Fargo and put her hands on her hips. "You didn't."

"I might have," Fargo said.

"You didn't warn them about the Indian?"

"It's a white man," Fargo said. "I went back out there and saw him but he got away."

"And you didn't think to tell me?" Belinda shook her head and brushed past. "So much for the two of us getting better acquainted."

Fargo watched her shapely behind sway from side to side. "Son of bitch," he said.

# 10

Artemis McWhertle had been placed facedown on the bed in a small room at the rear of the second floor. They had stripped him to the waist. He was groaning in pain and spittle dribbled from a corner of his mouth.

The arrow had caught him between the shoulder blades and penetrated so deep, Edna hadn't been able to pull it out or work it loose.

"That's another reason I came for you," she explained to Belinda. "I figured if anyone could cut it out, it was you."

Artemis opened his eyes. "Who's there?"

"It's me, cousin," Edna said. "I fetched Dr. Jackson like I told you I would."

"I don't want no female doc cuttin' on me," Artemis growled. "Where's Orville, anyhow? And Harold?"

"They went after Old Man Sawyer. Orville said as how he'd bury Sawyer for what he done to you."

"Blamed idiots. I'm lyin' here dyin' and they go to kill the man who killed me when I ain't even dead yet."

Fargo was leaning against a wall with his arms crossed. "Brains sure are scarce in these parts," he sympathized.

The woman who had ridden to the settlement with Edna glanced over sharply. She was Orville's wife, Mabel. She had sandy hair and cheeks that drooped and a body that made Fargo think of a dumpling. "Does this amuse you, Mr. Fargo? A fellow human bein' in torment?"

"I will admit, ma'am," Fargo replied, with a nod at Artemis, "that it couldn't have happened to a nicer jackass."

"Don't start," Belinda said to him. "We're here to help, not cause a fracas." She sat on the edge of the bed. "Artemis, can you hear me?"

"I got an arrow stuck in my back. I ain't deaf."

"I can dig this out but only with your consent. What do you say?"

"Go to hell."

"Tell me, Artemis," she said. "Does your chest hurt when you move?"

"Everything hurts," he grumpily responded.

"I mean a sharp pain now and then?"

"What if there is?"

Belinda turned to Edna and Mabel. "I was afraid that would be the case." She indicated the arrow. "Judging by the penetration and the angle it went in, there's a good chance the tip is dangerously close to his heart."

"Oh my," Edna said.

"You can't tell that just by lookin'," Mabel declared.

"True," Belinda said. "But if I'm right, the least little movement could kill him."

"You're tryin' to scare us," Mabel said, "so that Art will let you operate." Her thin lips pinched together. "I was against comin' for you, I'll have you know. It was all Edna's doin'."

"I imagined as much," Belinda said, and offered an encouraging smile to Edna. "Thank you for your confidence in me. It's a shame the rest of your family doesn't see things your way."

Artemis had been listening and said, "You ain't cuttin' on me, bitch. You hear me? Someone find Orville. He's cut on hogs and cows before. He can do me." He started to raise his head and cried out. Slumping, he said weakly, "That was the worst pain yet."

"I warned you," Belinda said.

"If there's a shovel handy," Fargo spoke up, "I'll dig the grave."

The women and Artemis looked at him in a mix of shock and outrage.

"I ain't dead yet!" Artemis spat.

"You will be soon enough," Fargo said. He deliberately laughed and nodded at Belinda. "Here you have a woman who studied for years to learn how to save people and you won't let her."

"I ain't lettin' no woman doctor me and that's all there is to it," Artemis said.

"We'll scrawl that on your tombstone," Fargo said.

Mabel stepped to the bed and put her hand on her in-law's shoulder. "Don't listen to him, Art. He's tryin' to get your goat."

"I ain't hankerin' to die."

"My man Orville will be here sooner or later and he'll have you right as rain," Mabel said.

"Maybe he won't come," Artemis said. "Maybe that crazy loon put an arrow in him, too."

"You could stick ten arrows in Orville and it wouldn't hardly phase him," Mabel said.

Artemis tried to look over his shoulder at the arrow, and groaned. "Doc?" he said weakly.

"I'm still here," Belinda said.

"Get it done."

"Art!" Mabel exclaimed.

Belinda bent over him. "I need to be clear on this. You want me to operate?"

"I do," Artemis affirmed.

"He does not," Mabel said.

"I do so, damn you," Artemis came close to shouting. He collapsed and moaned and whispered to Belinda, "You'd best hurry, Doc. I can feel myself fadin'."

"Don't do this, Art," Mabel said. "It'll make Orville awful mad."

"Orville ain't lyin' here dyin'," Artemis said.

Belinda picked her bag up from the floor and set it on the bed. She unfastened the snap and opened it and was reaching in when Mabel gripped her wrist.

"I won't allow it, you hear? Orville would take a switch to me if I let you."

"Please," Belinda said, trying to wrest free. "Every second is crucial."

"Leave her be, Mabel," Edna said. "She's here at my biddin', remember?"

"I don't care," Mabel said. "There's no way in Hades she's carvin' on him."

By then Fargo was behind her. He wrapped his arms around hers, pinning them to her side. Swinging her away from the bed, he forcibly half carried, half pushed her toward the door. "Enough is enough."

Mabel was livid. She swore and kicked and then grabbed the jambs on either side to prevent him from taking her out. "Let go of me, you son of a bitch!"

With a powerful wrench, Fargo forced her into the hall and gave her a push that sent her stumbling. She recovered her balance, whirled, and flew at him with her fists balled, screaming, "I will bust your face!"

Fargo took a step back. "Simmer down." But she was too mad to heed. She swung at his head and neck and he brought up his arms to defend himself. She wasn't puny and her punches hurt. He took ten or twelve wild blows and then she clipped him on the cheek. "Enough!" he warned her, and pushed her away.

Mabel swore and renewed her assault. "I'll teach you by God to lay a hand on me!"

Fargo slugged her. He held back—some—and caught her flush on the chin. She folded in her tracks, her eyes rolling up into her head. He caught her and carried her downstairs to the parlor and set her on the settee. He wasn't gentle about it.

A floorboard creaked behind him. Fargo spun, his hand dropping to his Colt, but it was only Edna McWhertle, wringing her hands.

"I saw what you did. She didn't leave you much choice."

Fargo rubbed his knuckles. "The bitch has a jaw like a rock."

Edna bit her lower lip and gazed up the stairs. "Doc Jackson shooed me out. Said as how she can handle it by her lonesome. I offered to heat water but she told me to make myself scarce."

"How much trouble will you get in for this?"

Edna shrugged. "Some, I reckon. Orville will be mad as can be. He'll want Harold to beat me but Harold might not if I talk to him sweet."

"He's beaten you before?"

"I'm his woman. He has the right."

"Hell," Fargo said.

"You're not married, I hear," Edna said. "You wouldn't know how it is."

"Why don't you explain it to me?"

Edna stepped to a chair and tiredly sank down. "A woman has to know her place. When she marries she promises to obey, and when she doesn't, it's up to her husband to set her right."

"Is that Harold talking? Or you?"

"Well, mostly it's him," Edna said. "When we got hitched I didn't think he'd be how he turned out. So stern, I mean. I think it's because he looks up to Orville and Orville beats Mabel all the time."

Fargo looked at the woman on the settee and frowned.

"I try to rein in my independent streak, as Harold calls it," Edna resumed, "but it's hard. I guess I'm just contrary by nature."

"I bet that's him talking again," Fargo said. "You're a grown woman. You have the right to do and say what you damn well please."

"I hear tell there are places where that's true," Edna said, "but it's not true hereabouts and it's sure not true in this house."

"I'm surprised you put up with it. I sure as hell wouldn't."

"Now see," Edna said, "that's because you're a man. But what else am I to do? He earns the money. And we have children. It's not as if I can pack them up and leave. Not that there hasn't been a time or two I didn't want to, after he got done hittin' me."

"You could find another man."

"Oh, Mr. Fargo," Edna said quietly. "I ain't much of a looker and I'm in my middle years. And with kids, besides? Most men wouldn't give me a first look, let alone a second."

Fargo didn't say anything.

"No, I'm stuck here. And it's not all bad. Harold and me have had some good times. It's just that I don't agree with how him and his kin treat the doc. She's a good woman. She cares about folks."

"Tell that to the jackasses who hate her."

Edna folded her hands in her lap. "It's not entirely them," she said.

"Who else, then?"

"Why, Charles T. Dogood, of course. That man hates her. He has hated her from the day she hung up her shingle and his hate has only gotten worse. You should hear how he talks about her. All the stuff he says behind her back. He's turned a lot of the folks in this county against her, and that's no lie."

"He doesn't want her taking his business."

"That's part of it," Edna said. "But there's more there, too."

"More how?"

"I'm not sure. But I've listened to him a lot. I have to, when he's talkin' to Harold and the rest. And it's more than hate that drives him. There is somethin' else but I don't know what." Edna wrung her hands. "I'm afraid Dogood will be madder than ever over me bringin' her to help Artemis. It wouldn't surprise me if he stirs folks up enough to run her and you plumb out of Coogan County."

"They're welcome to try," Fargo said.

# 11

After an hour Fargo got tired of sitting around. Edna had gone into the kitchen. Her children were asleep. There hadn't been a peep out of Belinda Jackson except once when she poked her head out to say she needed clean towels.

Fargo went out on the porch and stretched. Stars speckled the firmament and a brisk breeze stirred the maples and oaks. He leaned against a post and listened to the distant keening yip of a coyote. In the vicinity of the barn an owl hooted.

The Ovaro was dozing.

If he had any sense, Fargo told himself, he'd climb on and be out of the Ozarks before the new day was done. Orville McWhertle had been right in that this was none of his affair. Then again, he didn't like anyone telling him what he could or couldn't do, and he damn sure didn't like seeing Belinda treated the way they were treating her.

Then, too, Orville and Artemis had attacked him, and he never took kindly to anyone trying to pound him to a pulp or stick cold steel in him.

Add the crazy old buzzard who tried to skewer him with arrows, and Fargo felt he had several good reasons for sticking around.

Down on the road hooves rumbled. The riders turned in at the lane and came through the orchard, slowing as they neared the farmhouse. They didn't spot him in the shadows.

Orville was in front. Behind him came Harold and four others, all stamped from the family mold. Each and every one had a rifle in his scabbard. None, as near as Fargo could tell, wore a revolver.

It was Orville who noticed the Ovaro and blurted, "What in hell?" He tapped his spurs and brought his bay up next to the stallion. "Will you look at this?"

Harold and the rest came to a stop and Harold said, "Why do you reckon he came back?"

"I aim to find out," Orville declared, and started to swing his right leg up.

Fargo moved to the top of the steps, the light from the front window at his back, his hand on his Colt. "Stay right where you are."

Orville froze, then slowly lowered his leg and placed his huge hands on his saddle horn. "Mister, you've got a lot of gall."

"What are you doin' here?" Harold demanded. "I told you before to stay off my place."

"I brought Dr. Jackson," Fargo said.

Orville jerked upright and glared at the house. "That female doc is here too? What's she up to?"

"What do you think?" Fargo rejoined.

"Son of a bitch," Orville rasped. "How did she find out about Artemis?"

Harold brought his horse closer. "I didn't give her permission to go in my house. I'll have the law after her for trespassin'."

"Someone else asked her to come," Fargo said.

"Who?"

Fargo shrugged.

"I know who it was," Orville said, and glowered at Harold. "It's that woman of yours. Who else would of done it?"

"Edna knows better," Harold said, but not with a lot of conviction.

"Like hell. She's always goin' against your wishes. And she's always had a soft spot for the female sawbones. Now she went and brought her out here to tend to Art after you told her before we left she wasn't to do any such thing."

"I'll beat her black and blue if she did," Harold declared, and he went to dismount.

"Stay on your horse," Fargo warned. "All of you."

"What the hell?" Harold snapped. "You can't tell a man what to do on his own property and on his own horse."

"The doc's not to be bothered," Fargo said. "Until she's done no one is going in."

"There are six of us and only one of you. We won't be bluffed."

Orville spared Fargo having to answer by saying, "Use your noggin, Harold. He can slick that smoke wagon and put a bullet into each of us before we clear our rifles."

"How do we know he's that good?"

"How do we know he's not?" Orville countered. "We already saw how fast he is, and a man that's practiced that much is liable to be just as good at hittin' what he aims at."

Fargo was slightly impressed. Orville was more than a mountain of muscle; there was a brain in there somewhere.

"We could rush him all at once," Harold proposed.

"We're on our horses, you dimwit," Orville said. "Or do you expect him to wait until all of us have climbed down to start shootin'?"

"Don't be callin' me names, cousin," Harold said. "I hate it when you treat me like I'm dumb."

"And I hate it when you're dumb, so we're even," Orville said.

To take their minds off any notion of attacking him, Fargo asked, "Did you find Old Man Sawyer?"

"No," Orville said glumly, "we did not. And we went all over those woods for a mile around his cabin."

"What can have gotten into him, puttin' an arrow into Artemis like that?" one of the other men brought up.

Orville nodded at Fargo. "The scout, here, thinks as how Sawyer has rabies."

"The hell you say."

"I thought rabies just makes you thirsty and then your muscles get stiff and you can't walk and you die," said another man.

"Maybe he just went loco," suggested a third, "killin' all his animals like he done."

The front door opened and Belinda came out. She put a hand to the small of her back and arched it and came to the rail. "It took some doing but I extracted the arrow," she announced. "I've stitched him up and given him a sedative. Your cousin Artemis will live."

Instead of expressing gratitude, Orville stabbed a finger at her. "Don't think this changes anythin'. It doesn't. You don't pull up stakes, and soon, you won't like what happens."

"Not even a little bit," Harold gleefully chimed in.

Belinda sighed and looked at Fargo. "If this hasn't persuaded them, what will?"

"This," Fargo said, and patted his Colt.

"I pray it doesn't come to that," she said quietly.

Orville rumbled in his chest like an angry bear. "You don't

want it to come to that then light a shuck." He began to dismount. "I reckon it's safe for us go in now, boys."

Taking hold of Belinda's arm, Fargo moved aside so the farmers could go by. Orville and Harold made it a point to glare. The others didn't seem to hate as much. As the door slammed behind them, Belinda bowed her head and wearily rubbed a temple.

"I'm beginning to wonder why I bother."

"Saving that no-account's life doesn't count?" Fargo said.

"It goes deeper than that. I've tried and I've tried to win these people over and so many of them continue to reject me. I'm at my wit's end."

Fargo leaned close and said into her ear, "You've had a long day. You need to relax."

She looked at him and his mouth quirked. "Do I, indeed? And I suppose you have an idea how I should go about it?"

"It will curl your toes," Fargo said.

Belinda laughed and pecked him on the cheek. "Thank you, kind sir. You have perked my spirits."

"Let's get you home and we'll perk something else."

"Oh my." Belinda did more laughing. "I have to fetch my bag and we'll be on our way."

"I'll go with you."

"There's no need," she said. "They won't harm me after what I just—"

From inside the farmhouse came a scream. Not a normal scream, if a scream could ever be called normal. It was a scream of pure and total terror, torn from the throat of the screamer. It rose to an earsplitting shriek and ended in a gurgle.

"My God," Belinda said, her hand on her throat. "That sounded like Edna." She was through the door before Fargo could stop her.

Thinking that Harold must be beating his wife, Fargo darted after her. He was on her heels when they came to the foot of the stairs.

Harold and Orville and the other men were already there, staring up uneasily.

"What's going on?" Belinda asked. "Why did Edna scream like that?"

"She went up to check on Abigail," Harold said, "and then we heard that awful cry." He bounded up the stairs and everyone else followed suit.

Fargo came last. He glanced in the parlor and saw Mabel still out on the settee. He'd forgotten about her. When she came around and told Orville he'd hit her, there would be hell to pay. He'd better be gone before then.

The farmers and the physician stopped at a closed door. "This is our bedroom," Harold said. He tried to open it and said angrily, "It's bolted on the inside."

"You have a bolt on your bedroom door?" Orville said.

"So the kids can't come barging in on us." Harold pounded and shook the door. "Edna? Are you all right? What the hell was that? And why is the door bolted?"

In the room someone whimpered.

"Was that her?" one of the men asked.

"Edna?" Harold hollered louder, and shook the door more violently. "Let us in, you hear?"

"Break it down," Belinda said.

"Like hell," Harold replied. "Doors cost money and I can't afford to replace it."

"But your wife is in trouble."

"It would serve her right, sendin' for you without my say-so."

"Oh, hell," Fargo said. Shoving Harold aside, he raised his boot to kick the door but just then there was a scraping noise and the door was jerked open.

Edna stumbled out. The left side of her neck had been torn open, and she had a hand over it to stem the flow of blood. Not much was coming out although a lot already had; the front and back of her dress were stained crimson. She looked at her husband and gasped, "Harold!"

Harold was rooted in shock. "What in the world?" he blurted. She fell into his arms and would have fallen to the floor had Orville not sprang to help. "What could have done this?"

Fargo tried to see into the bedroom but too many people were in his way.

Uttering a groan, Edna passed out.

"Let's set her down," Orville said, and they eased her onto her back.

Belinda tried to get between them, saying, "I need to have a look at her. She needs immediate treatment."

"You've done enough," Harold barked, and grabbed her to prevent her from intervening.

Fargo coiled to defend her but suddenly one of the other men let out a cry of horror.

"God in heaven! Look!"

A girl of ten or so was in the doorway. She wore a plain white cotton dress and had long brown hair. Her face was twisted in savage fury—and she was foaming at the mouth.

# 12

Everyone turned to stone.

The girl looked at each of them. Her eyes were so bloodshot, the whites were red. Her pupils were dilated. With each breath she took her nose flared, and all the while froth bubbled around her lips and dribbled down her chin and neck.

"Abigail?" Harold said.

The girl hissed and hooked her fingers into claws. Several of the men, including Orville, took an involuntary step back, and one man gasped.

"Abby?" Harold said again. "This is your pa. What in heaven's name has happened to you?" He reached for her.

"No!" Belinda cried.

It was too late. Abigail sprang and bit down on her father's fingers. Harold screeched, there was a *crunch*, and the girl bit the ends of two of the fingers off. She pulled back, the fingertips jutting from her teeth, and did something that made even Fargo's blood chill: she smiled.

Harold clutched his hand, blood pumping from the stumps, and blubbered gibberish.

"God preserve us!" another McWhertle exclaimed.

Abigail spat the fingers out. Some of the foam flew in small drops onto the man's arm and he recoiled as if the drops were the plague.

"Abby?" Belinda reached for her but the girl ducked under her grasp. "Grab her!" she cried.

The girl ducked under Orville's halfhearted attempt to grasp her and passed the others. She was incredibly quick.

Fargo tried, and missed.

"Catch her, Skye!" Belinda said. "We can't let her get away."

Abigail flew down the hall and Fargo ran in pursuit. He reached the top of the stairs and saw her at the bottom. She glanced up and gave him another of those awful smiles, and then she raced off. He took the stairs three at a bound. She had left the front door open and he sped out onto the porch. To his left a small white form was streaking toward the barn. Leaping over the rail, he pumped his legs. He was considered fleet of foot and had taken part in a few footraces and done well but the girl was inhuman. She reached the barn and disappeared inside.

When he got there he stopped. She had already bitten her mother's neck and bit off her father's fingers; he'd be damned if he would let her bite him, too.

Fargo placed his hand on his Colt, then took it off. He wouldn't shoot her if he could help it. Warily, he entered. The barn smelled of horses and cows and straw. He looked for a lantern but it was too dark to see one. He cautiously advanced down the aisle. In a stall a horse nickered. "Abigail?" he said. "We want to help you."

From somewhere deeper in came a hiss.

Fargo's skin crawled. He would take on anyone man-to-man or man-to-beast. But this? Something terrible had happened to this girl. Something had changed her. He remembered Old Man Sawyer and his skin crawled anew. Sweat broke out. Whatever it was, he realized, it must be contagious. Which meant if the girl bit him—

Something moved at the end of the aisle.

Fargo felt his mouth go dry. If it was rabies there was no cure. Everyone who came down with it died. He licked his lips and moved more slowly, his body a taut spring, ready to dodge or backpedal. "Abigail," he said softly. "I'm a friend. Can you understand?"

Another hiss told him she couldn't.

Fargo walked on eggshells. A thump to his left caused him to whirl but it was only a horse in a stall. He edged forward. Suddenly there was the rasp of leather hinges and a door at the back was flung wide and a white form darted out. He hurtled after her.

The cool night air chilled the sweat on his body. Ahead, the white figure was plunging into a field of corn. He ran to the edge of the field, and stopped. It would be folly for him to go in after her. The stalks were so tightly spaced, the rows so close together, that she could come out of nowhere and sink her teeth into him before he could stop her.

Fargo stood there, debating. Other than slight rustling the corn was still, the dark ominous. He imagined her waiting for him, her red eyes blazing, her mouth dripping foam.

Voices reached him, and he turned. Light filled the barn. Another moment and Orville McWhertle and two others emerged, Orville carrying a lantern above his head. They spotted him and came over.

"She went in there?" one of the cousins asked.

Fargo nodded.

"Did you ever see the like in all your born days?" asked the other man.

Fargo shook his head.

"It's rabies," Orville declared. "It has to be. First Sawyer and now sweet little Abby."

"She didn't seem so sweet to me," said one of the men.

"Do you think it's rabies, mister?" the other one asked Fargo.

"I don't know."

"What else can it be?" Orville said.

"I'm no doctor," Fargo said, "but I've heard that to catch it you have to be bit."

"So?"

"So when did Old Man Sawyer bite Abigail?"

The McWhertles looked at one another.

"God Almighty," the second man said. "It must be he's sneakin' around bitin' folks."

"But why her?" Fargo said.

"Rabid folk don't need a why," Orville said. "They just bite. She's been laid up with a fever for a couple of days now. He must've bit her three or four days ago."

"How long does it take after you're bit for the rabies to turn you mad?" the first man asked.

"How the hell would I know," Orville said.

"Dr. Jackson does, I bet," Fargo mentioned.

"Big help she'll be," Orville said. "There's nothin' she can do and you damn well know it."

"Let's go ask her," proposed the second man.

"What about Abigail?" asked the first, gesturing at the corn.

"Do you want to go in there, Abner?" Orville said.

"Lord help me, I sure as hell do not."

"Do you, Clyde?"

"No. I got me a wife and kids of my own. I don't want my blood tainted and have to be put down like a dog or a coon."

"How about you, scout? Why didn't you go in after her? Could it be you're scared?"

"I'm not a fool," Fargo said. "I'll wait for daylight and track her down."

They turned and started for the barn and were halfway there when Harold came out the rear door with a towel wrapped around his right hand and his arm clasped to his chest. The towel was stained red. "Where's my daughter? Why ain't you after her?"

"She got into the corn, cousin," Orville said.

"So? We'll take a lantern and go find her. If we spread out we can cover the whole field."

"Not me," Abner said.

"Me neither," Clyde said. "I ain't lookin' to be bit." He stared at the red towel. "How are you feelin', Harold? It get into your blood yet?"

"What?" Harold said.

"Why, the rabies, you dunce," Clyde said. "What did you reckon was the matter with her?"

"The rabies?" Harold said, and his face drained white. He, too, looked at the towel and said, "Oh God. I didn't think of that."

"Edna and you both will get it now," Orville said.

"We don't know it's rabies," Fargo remarked, but no one paid him any mind.

"It must have been Old Man Sawyer." Harold came to the same conclusion as his kin. "He must of bit her days ago. But when? And where? She's been close to home the whole time. And she never mentioned runnin' into him." He ran his unhurt hand over his head. "You'd think she'd have mentioned a thing like bein' bit."

Clyde cleared his throat. "We'll have to . . ." He stopped. "What's that word? Oh, yeah, I remember now. We'll have to quarantine you and your missus so when you take to foamin', you don't bite anyone else and spread it worse."

"Quarantine?" Harold repeated, stunned.

"Let's go talk to the lady sawbones," Orville said. "As much as I hate to admit it, she probably knows more about rabies than anyone, even Charlie Dogood."

Fargo followed. As he was about to enter the barn he glanced over his shoulder and thought he glimpsed a small white form crouched in the corn. He blinked, and it was gone.

The men were somber as they filed into the house and up the

stairs. Belinda had gotten Edna onto the bed. Edna was unconscious and Belinda was stitching her neck wound with a long needle. She looked up as they appeared in the doorway. "That's far enough."

"This is my house and she's my wife," Harold said. "I can come in if I want."

"I can't afford to be distracted," Belinda said. "And I need you or someone else to heat water and bring the pot upstairs. I have to clean this wound to prevent infection."

"What about the rabies?" Orville asked. "What can you do about that?"

"I don't think it is," Belinda said.

"Why? We all saw that girl foamin' at the mouth. And your friend, Fargo, said he saw Old Man Sawyer doin' the same."

Belinda paused with her needle inserted in a strip of flesh. "Listen to me. I can't be disturbed right now. But I'll simply say that it's my understanding that when a person contracts rabies, by the time they're foaming at the mouth, they're also experiencing seizures and paralysis. In other words, they're incapacitated to the point where they can't go around attacking others."

"Inca-what?" Harold asked.

"They can't move much," Belinda clarified. "Now please. If I'm to have any hope of saving your wife, I need that water and I need privacy." She went to bend over Edna but looked up again. "Oh. And Harold. As soon as I'm finished with Edna, I'll take a look at your hand."

"I'm fine," Harold said. "The bleedin' has mostly stopped."

The McWhertles turned and descended the stairs, their voices fading as they neared the kitchen.

Fargo leaned against the jamb and folded his arms. "Is there anything I can do?"

Belinda glanced over and smiled. "Not at the moment." She bent to the needle. "I forgot to ask them. What happened to Abigail?"

"She ducked into the corn. I'll go after her at first light."

"There are two of them out there now," Belinda said worriedly. "And despite what I told the others, to be perfectly honest, I'm not sure it's not rabies. I haven't had any experience with the disease."

"I wouldn't tell them that," Fargo said.

"No, I won't. We don't want a panic on our hands," Belinda

said. "Although now that I think about it, I should send riders to warn everyone to be on the lookout for anyone or anything that shows the symptoms."

"Any advice you can give me for when I go after the girl?" Fargo asked.

"Yes," Belinda said. "Don't get bit."

# 13

The golden orb of the sun blazed the misty eastern horizon when Fargo stepped into the stirrups and reined the Ovaro toward the cornfield. He'd slept on the settee, or tried to, and had a fitful night. He kept waking up at the slightest sound. It didn't help that Harold McWhertle refused to bolt the doors in case Abigail came back. Orville argued that he was putting their lives at risk but Harold refused to give in.

Belinda had stayed up in the bedroom with Edna so Harold slept in another bedroom by himself. His kids he put down in the root cellar. The rest of the McWhertles sprawled wherever they saw fit.

No one else was up when Fargo roused and went to the kitchen. He'd kindled the stove and helped himself to coffee left over from the day before.

Now here he was, off to find the possibly rabid spitfire.

The morning air was brisk but that would soon change.

He rode around the barn and crossed to the corn and drew rein. He had a choice. He could track her through the corn, which could take a month of Sundays, or he could circle and try to find where she'd left the corn for parts unknown. He chose the second.

Reining right, Fargo went along the perimeter to the corner and reined left. The only tracks he saw were those of a rabbit and an opossum. He went another thirty feet, and stopped. There, in a patch of bare dirt, was the partial print of a small naked foot. It pointed toward woods that covered a nearby hill.

Fargo tapped his spurs. Out of habit he loosened the Colt in its holster.

At daybreak the trees were always alive with the warbling of birds. Wrens twittered and sparrows chirped.

Shafts of sunlight dappled a clearing where a doe and a fawn grazed.

Fargo was finding it hard to spot sign. The girl was a sprout, barely seventy pounds, and the ground was covered with leaves. Half the time he had to guess which way she'd gone and twice he had to backtrack. By the middle of the morning he'd traveled barely a mile and had yet to see her. She'd been meandering all over the place. It was a wonder, he reflected, that a coyote or a bear hadn't stumbled on her. Then again, one whiff and an animal was likely to run the other way.

A blue ribbon of water gleamed amid the greens and browns. Fargo came to a small creek and dismounted. While the Ovaro drank he scanned the countryside for a patch of white. The girl was nowhere to be seen. He sighed and turned toward the stallion.

Not ten yards away stood Abigail, her small body in a crouch, her fingers claws, her eyes as red as the night before, and her chin flecked with froth.

The instant Fargo saw her, she hissed and charged. He side-stepped and she flew past, only to wheel on a heel and come at him again. He pivoted, hooked her legs with his boot, and sent her tumbling. But she rolled and was on her feet in the bat of an eye and came at him again, her teeth bared.

"Damn it, girl." Fargo dodged, spun, dodged again. She flew past and he grabbed her shoulders, only to have to snatch his hands away when she snapped at them.

Abigail paused, her wiry frame hunched, more froth oozing from her open mouth.

"I don't want to have to hurt you," Fargo said, knowing full well she couldn't understand.

Hissing, Abigail launched herself at his legs. Fargo tried to dart aside but she lunged and wrapped her arms around his left thigh. Her teeth closed on his buckskins.

Fargo pushed with all his strength and the girl went tumbling. He bent to examine his leg; a horror welling up subsided. But her teeth weren't sharp enough to rip through buckskin. His flesh hadn't been punctured. He smiled in relief and looked up.

Abigail was gone.

Fargo looked right and left and there she was—stalking toward the Ovaro. "No!" he cried, and ran at her. She skipped away and hissed. He grabbed at her hair but she was too quick and slipped under his arm and flew into the woods.

"Damn it."

Fargo gave chase. He was confident she wouldn't get away, not in broad daylight.

Abigail was moving flat out, her small lithe form a blur. She vaulted a boulder with ease and skirted a small pine.

Fargo went around it and nearly ran into her. She had stopped and spun and was waiting for him. This time she leaped at his throat, not his legs. He got a hand up and she snapped at it. He closed his fingers on her neck and felt spittle under his palm. The girl screeched and bit at his wrist but she couldn't quite reach it. Seizing the front of her dress, he forced her onto her back on the ground. She kicked. She clawed. She uttered a wail of fury.

Fargo's rope was on his saddle. He needed it but he didn't dare let go of her. Instead, he dragged her toward the Ovaro. She resisted with all the might in her small body. Whether it was the disease or her rage or both but she was stronger by far than any normal girl. It was all he could do to hold on to her.

Her foot caught him close to his groin. Her nails raked his cheek.

"Damn it," Fargo said again. The longer they struggled, the more the risk of his being bitten. He had to end it. He cocked his fist but he couldn't bring himself to hit her.

It was stupid but there it was.

Abigail twisted violently. She craned her neck and slashed with her teeth.

Fargo felt a sting. She'd broken the skin on a knuckle and it was bleeding. She went to bite him again and he threw her to the ground. He didn't mean to hurt her, not severely, and was surprised when she went limp.

"Abigail?" Fargo said, suspecting a trick. He nudged her with his boot but she didn't react. Bending, he gripped her by the arm and pulled. Again, nothing. With great care he gripped her shoulders and raised her partway, and saw the rock. It was melon sized, the part he could see that wasn't buried. When he flung her, she'd hit her head, and the rock was spattered with scarlet.

"Hell." Fargo bent to examine her, and caught himself. Going to the Ovaro, he got his rope. It took some doing to cut some off

73

even though his Arkansas toothpick was razor sharp. He tied her wrists behind her back and then tied her ankles. He also removed his bandanna and gagged her. Only then did he examine the wound. She had a gash but it didn't appear to be life threatening. Satisfied, he tied her belly down over his saddle and climbed on.

The farm was quiet when he arrived.

Belinda Jackson was seated on the porch steps, drinking coffee from a china cup. The instant she saw him she was on her feet and hurried over.

"You did it!"

Fargo showed her his knuckle. "She bit me."

Belinda took his hand. "It's not deep. Did you bleed much? No? Then I wouldn't worry."

"Where is everyone?"

"Edna and Harold are up in their bedroom. She hasn't come around and I insisted he stay in bed for the time being and rest. But damn, he's a difficult patient."

"The others?"

"They're still here . . ."

She got no further. The front door opened and out strode Orville, Abner, and Clyde. They came down the steps and Orville gently lifted Abigail from the saddle.

"Jesus, mister," Abner said. "What in hell did you do to her?"

"She hit her head on a rock," Fargo explained.

"Get her inside," Belinda directed. "We'll put her in her own bed."

Orville turned, then looked at Fargo. "For what it's worth, I'm obliged. You didn't have to do this. She ain't your kin."

Fargo nodded. They all went in and he wearily climbed down and tied the reins off. He could use some coffee himself. He ambled to the kitchen and was delighted to find a half-full pot, plenty hot. He filled a cup to the brim and sat at the table with his back to the wall so he could see the hallway and the back door, both. He'd taken several grateful swallows when the doorway filled with a man-mountain.

"I meant what I said even though I shouldn't even be talkin' to you. My wife has been naggin' me all night to stomp you for hittin' her."

"Are you turning over a new leaf?"

Orville pulled out the chair across from him. "You don't give an inch, do you?"

"Not usually, no," Fargo admitted.

"Well, I'm bein' honest with you. My kin mean a lot to me. But I guess you noticed."

Fargo grunted.

"So when someone does us a favor, I remember it."

"Do me a favor, then," Fargo said.

"Name it."

"Quit being an ass about Jackson. She's a damn good sawbones, whether you like her or not."

Orville's jaw twitched. "You push and you push. The best I can say is that I'll ponder on it some."

"It's a start," Fargo said, then stated, "I just don't savvy why you're so fond of Dogood."

"Charlie has been helpin' folks in these parts for twenty years or more," Orville said. "He's been to our house for supper more times than I can count."

"That's cause to hate Jackson?"

"There's more to it."

"I would really like to know," Fargo said.

Orville frowned and shifted in his chair. "He asked us to sort of run her off if we could."

"And you agreed?"

"Not in so many words," Orville said. "But like I just told you, he's more than a patent medicine man to us. He's a friend. This doc doesn't like him. She's said as much. Hell, she hadn't been in Ketchum Falls a week when she was callin' Charlie a quack and such. She had the gall to try to give us the notion that we should drive *him* off. That didn't sit well. It didn't sit well at all."

Fargo sighed.

"What we've got here is feudin' docs with us caught in the middle," Orville said.

"Dogood's not a doctor."

"As far as we're concerned he is," Orville said. "He's healed more of us than you can count."

Fargo wondered about that. Most people healed naturally, given enough time.

"I've been thinkin' about it, though," Orville had gone on, "and with this rabies business, maybe it's best she sticks around. For the time bein'," he amended.

"Your friend Dogood won't like that."

"It's rabies," Orville said. "Even he can't do anythin' about rabies. There's only one way to deal with it and I've called a meetin' of all the kinfolk for tonight to talk it over."

"I don't follow you," Fargo said.

"What do you do with a rabid dog or a rabid coon? You put it down, is what. You put a bullet in its head."

"So?"

"So that's what I'm goin' to propose we do with everybody who's been bit. We're goin' to kill every last one."

Fargo stared at his knuckle and didn't say anything.

# 14

Fargo figured a couple of dozen people would show. He stopped counting at sixty.

By sundown there were so many horses and buckboards and buggies that the front yard looked like the gathering for a church social.

He planted himself in a rocking chair in a corner of the porch.

The McWhertles were gabbing and some smiled now and then and occasionally someone laughed but overall it was a somber gathering. A lot of nervous stares were cast at the house.

Orville came out and stood at the rail. Abner and Clyde flanked him. When Orville raised his huge arms, silence fell.

A boy who was whistling was told to shush. Two small girls were made to stop scampering about.

"It warms my heart that so many of you came," Orville began. "But it saddens me why we're here."

The screen door creaked and Belinda emerged. She appeared tired and worn and her bangs hung in wisps over her forehead. She leaned against the wall and smiled tiredly at Fargo. He nodded. He'd wanted to talk to her all afternoon but never got the chance. She'd hovered over her patients and wouldn't let anyone come anywhere near them.

"I reckon by now all of you have heard," Orville continued with his speech. "Old Man Sawyer went loco. No one could figure out why. Now little Abby has gone loco, too, and we've figured out what it is. They both have rabies."

"Hold on," Belinda interrupted, and moved to the rail. "I'm not entirely convinced it *is* rabies. The symptoms don't match the disease as I understand it."

Orville frowned and addressed his kin. "Everyone here knows Doc Jackson, I take it? Edna asked her to come out to treat Abby and then Abby bit Edna and Harold and now the lady sawbones is

77

treatin' all three." He looked at her. "You say that you can't be sure that what ails them is rabies, is that right?"

"I need to do tests."

"Answer the question," Orville said.

"No, I can't say for sure."

"But you can't say for sure it ain't, either, can you?" Orville asked.

"Well, no, but—"

Orville held up a hand and turned to his listeners. "You heard her, folks. She's a doctor but she can't say one way or the other. I'll be nice and not comment on how poor a doc a person has to be not to know rabies when she sees it—"

"Here now," Belinda cut in. "I won't have you belittle me in front of all these people."

"Seems to me," Orville said slyly, "that you're belittlin' yourself."

Smiles and grins showed that a lot of the McWhertles agreed with him.

"Medicine is a science," Belinda raised her voice. "We learn by experience, by trial and error. We catalogue symptoms and compare them to a patient's condition and thereby diagnose with some degree of accuracy."

"Big words," Orville said. "But while you're doin' all that cataloguin' and comparin', people are bein' bit and foamin' at the mouth."

"We don't know that the bites are the cause," Belinda persisted.

"What else would cause it?" Orville challenged her. "What else made little Abigail tear out part of her own ma's neck? What else made the girl chomp off the ends of her own pa's fingers?"

"I keep telling you I don't know yet."

"Yet," Orville repeated, and gave his relatives a pointed look. "Tell us, Dr. Jackson. How long will it be before you *do* know?"

"There's no way to predict. I'll send blood and saliva samples to a chemist but it could take him weeks to get back to me. In the meantime the best I can do is mark their progress and see if any new symptoms develop and maybe then I'll have the clues I need."

"Maybe then?" Orville said. He motioned at those in the yard. "And what are we supposed to do in the meantime? Twiddle our thumbs while more and more of us take to hissin' and bitin' and runnin' around all crazed?"

Belinda faced the crowd. "If you're asking my advice, here it is. Stay in your homes. Keep your children and pets inside. I'll sort this out. I'll promise you."

"How long do we stay inside?" a man said. "A week? Two weeks? Who's goin' to feed our cows and our chickens and tend our fields?"

"Stay in our homes!" another man guffawed. "Should we hide under our beds, too?"

Some of them laughed.

"It's only until we have a handle on the situation," Belinda said.

"We already do, missy," a middle-aged woman in a bonnet told her. "It's rabies. It spreads when someone is bit. All we have to do is keep from bein' bit and we'll be fine."

Orville seized the moment. "And the only way to be sure we're not bit is to round up those who have been and put them out of their misery."

"What?" Belinda said.

Fargo cleared his throat. "He wants to shoot everyone who was bitten."

"What?" Belinda said again, turning to Orville. "Are you insane?"

"No, I ain't," Orville replied, "and I aim to keep it that way."

"But you can't just kill them. What if it's not rabies? They might recover."

"Can you promise us they will?" Orville demanded. "Can you promise us no one else will come down with it?"

From out of the throng came a gruff, "No, she can't! All she can do is make empty promises." And out of their midst strolled Charles T. Dogood. He came to the porch and faced those in the yard and held his arms up. "Good people. All of you know me. All of you know how long and how tirelessly I have worked for the welfare of everyone in this community."

"That's true, Charlie," a man hollered.

"What do you say we should do?" another asked.

Dogood squared his shoulders and puffed out his chest. "Friends, I'll be honest. As much as I would like to say I have a cure for rabies, I don't. No one does. It saddens my heart that I'm powerless to help you when you need help the most."

"That's all right, Charlie," an old woman said. "No one expects you to be a miracle worker."

"Thank you, Mildred," Dogood said. "But before I offer my advice I want to be clear. I don't want anyone to accuse me of bias." He paused to let that sink in. "It's no secret that I don't see eye to eye with our esteemed female physician. It's not just that she's female, as some would have you believe.

"I'm sure most of the women here can attest that I don't begrudge any woman her sex. No, the reason Dr. Jackson and I have been at odds is because from the day she stepped foot in Ketchum Falls she has tried to turn you against me. You've all heard her attacks, I'm sure. She's tried to convince you that the medicines I sell don't work when there are many here who can attest to the fact they do. She's tried to persuade you that she's a better healer—"

"She's no such thing," a woman cried.

"—thank you, Clarinda. But as I was saying, she claims to be a better healer but when has she ever healed anyone my medicines couldn't?" Dogood shook his head. "No, far be it for me to level an unjust charge against someone, yet that is precisely what she has been doing."

The looks thrown at Belinda weren't friendly. "Hold on, now," she said to Dogood. "Perhaps I have suggested once or twice that you're not the miracle worker you pretend to be but that's hardly an unjust charge."

"Then you admit trying to turn people against me?" Dogood said.

"You're putting words in my mouth."

"But, madam," Dogood said with oily grace, "you put the words there, not I."

Muttering broke out.

Dogood turned back to his listeners. "I bear the woman no malice. She's misguided, is all. She thinks she knows better than you who you should go to when you're ill."

"I do not," Belinda said, but no one appeared to hear her.

"You still haven't told us what you think we should do," a man reminded Dogood.

"Friends," the patent medicine man said gravely, "I wouldn't presume to tell you to do anything. With your gracious consent, however, I'm willing to offer my advice."

"Offer away," Abner said.

"Very well." Dogood hooked his thumbs in his vest. "It seems to me this community is at a crossroads. The question you need to ask yourselves is this. Do you want a healer who has only your best interests at heart and can treat you for ailments that medical science admits it can't? Or do you want a healer who thinks because she went to medical school, she knows better than everyone? A woman who plainly believes she has the God-given right to tell you how to think and what to do."

"I never said any such thing!" Belinda exclaimed.

"You've asked them to get rid of me, have you not?" Dogood countered. "And before you answer, I remind you, madam, that they've heard you with their own ears."

"You're turning my words against me," Belinda said.

"If you want my advice," Dogood said to the others, "you should seriously consider whether having her around is worth it. After all, she's a disrupting element. Instead of working with you, as I do, to build a better community, she spends her time enticing you to turn against me."

"She has her nerve," Clarinda said.

"I ask you to consider whether we wouldn't be better off without *her*," Dogood said. "And if you do, perhaps now is the time to show her how you feel."

"Show her in what way, Charlie?" a man asked.

"Why, I should think it would be obvious. Make her leave but be civilized about it. Make her pack her things and load her buggy and go. Don't tar and feather her as some have proposed."

"She deserves tarrin'," someone called out.

"Might teach her to hold her tongue," a woman shouted.

"Now, now," Dogood said soothingly. "The poor woman can't help how she is. You can't punish someone for bein' who they are."

"We can if we want to," a woman cried.

"It would serve her right, tarrin' and featherin' her," asserted a white-haired matron. "Maybe it would teach her to be a little more humble."

"Humble?" Belinda angrily exploded. "When have I ever treated any of you with anything but the utmost respect?"

"You only think of yourself," a man said.

A companion on his left nodded. "You've been a thorn in our side long enough. It's high time we got rid of you, like Charlie says."

"Leave me out of this, good people," Dogood said. "If you run her out it must be your decision."

"I'm for it," the woman in the bonnet said. "Who else? A show of hands?"

Nearly every arm was elevated.

Orville broke his long silence with, "Anyone who doesn't want to be part of this is welcome to leave or go inside and wait until it's over." He pointed at several men. "There are old timbers lyin' out back of the barn that will do." He pointed at a couple more. "And there should be tar in the small shed by the chicken coop."

"That coop's right handy," Abner said, "seein' as how we'll need a lot of feathers, too."

"Surely you wouldn't," Belinda said to them, aghast.

"Lady," Clyde said, "we're about to run you out of here tied to a rail."

# 15

Fargo had listened to enough. He rose out of the chair with his Colt in his hand.

Abner and Clyde seized Belinda Jackson. She cried out and struggled and some in the crowd laughed. Everyone was so intent on her, they didn't notice Fargo until he was behind Orville McWhertle and jammed the Colt's muzzle against the back of Orville's head. "Let her go."

Orville stiffened and started to turn back but caught himself. "You again."

"I won't say it twice."

Abner and Clyde were glaring and still holding on to Belinda.

"He's bluffin'," Clyde declared.

"Sure is," Abner agrees. "He knows if he shoots you, we'll kill him dead."

"Maybe you will and maybe you won't," Fargo said, "but Orville won't be around to see it."

Several men at the front of the gathering moved toward the porch.

"No!" Orville commanded, and they stopped. "I know how this man is. He's not bluffing. I won't have my brains blown out because you think he is."

"What do you want us to do, then?" Abner asked.

"Release her," Orville said.

"Like hell I will," Clyde said. "We're runnin' her out and we'll do the same to him, besides."

There were murmurs of agreement from the rest of the assembled McWhertles.

Fargo shot Clyde. In the blink of an eye he sent a slug into Clyde's right shoulder and jammed the muzzle against Orville again.

Clyde was jolted by the impact and lost his hold on Belinda. Stumbling against the rail, he clutched it for support and wailed, "I'm shot! I'm shot!"

Again some of the men started forward. Again Orville hollered.

"Stand where you are, damn you! Didn't you just learn anythin'?"

"Oh, God, it hurts," Clyde whimpered, his hand on the wound. "Someone help me."

"I will," Belinda said, "if Abner, here, will let go of me."

"He doesn't," Fargo said, "and he takes a bullet, too."

Abner jerked his hands from her.

Belinda turned to Clyde.

"No," Fargo said. "Fetch your bag. We're lighting a shuck."

"But he's hurt," Belinda said. "It's my job to help those who suffer. And then there's Abby and Edna and Harold. They need me."

"Use your damn head," Fargo said. "Look at them." He gestured at the yard.

Nearly every face mirrored some degree of resentment or hate, the women included.

"After all I've done for them," Belinda said quietly.

"You've tried to help us," Orville conceded. "But we didn't ask you to. We don't want your help, woman, now or ever. You can't seem to get that through your head."

"Fetch your bag," Fargo said again. He wasn't sure how long he could hold the clan at bay. There was bound to be a hothead or two who wouldn't let a little thing like common sense stand in the way of getting themselves killed. "Fetch it *now.*"

Belinda nodded and hurried in.

"This won't end it," Orville said. "Convince her to leave Ketchum Falls or it will get ugly."

"You come after her," Fargo said, "and you have no idea how ugly."

"Look how many of us there are. You can't fight all of us."

"There will be a lot less," Fargo said.

It took Belinda ungodly long. Some in the crowd looked ready to rush the porch when she finally emerged with her black bag in hand.

"Sorry it took so long. I was checking on Abigail and Edna. They're both sleeping peacefully and neither has a fever."

"Would they have a fever if it was rabies?" Orville asked.

"Usually but not always. Sometimes it takes weeks or months before all the symptoms show. But as I told you before, I'm not convinced it is rabies."

"If not, what?"

"If you give me time I'm confident I can find out."

"Don't listen to her," Dogood said. "She knows full well it's rabies but she doesn't want to admit she can't be of any use."

"Were I you, you son of a bitch," Fargo said, "I'd keep my mouth shut."

Dogood's Adam's-apple bobbed.

"This is how we're going to do it," Fargo said to Orville. "Have your kin move over by the barn. Every last one. They don't, I'll shoot you. Then the doc and you and me will walk to our horses. Anyone tries to stop us, I'll shoot you. Once we're on, you're to step back with your hands in the air. Try any tricks, anything at all—"

"And you shoot me," Orville finished.

"You can do that?" Belinda said. "Shoot an unarmed man?"

"Lady," Orville answered before Fargo could, "this friend of yours could drop me dead and not care a whit."

"Is that true?" Belinda asked.

"Now's not the time." Fargo jabbed Orville with the Colt. "Get them moving."

Many were reluctant but they did as Orville told them. Only after they were clear across the yard did Fargo say, "Let's go. You first. Down the steps."

"I won't forget this," Orville said.

"Do I give a damn?" Fargo jabbed him. "Get going. Belinda, stay close."

"I hate leaving my patients."

"Would you rather be tarred and feathered?"

That shut her up.

Orville moved slowly, careful to keep his arms out from his sides. Once he was clear of the overhang, he raised them in the air. As they crossed the yard he cleared his throat. "If you know what's good for you, you'll both be gone from this county by this time tomorrow."

"I'm not going anywhere," Belinda said. "Can't you get it through your head that this is my home? I intend to spend the rest of my life here."

"You're a fool, woman."

"One of us is," Belinda said. "And don't forget. A lot of people in Coogan County like me. They want me to stay. The Barnabys, the Tibbetts, the Weavers. I could name a dozen more. They won't take kindly to you doing me harm."

"Like your gun hand friend said to me a minute ago," Orville responded, "do I give a damn?"

"You better, or you could end up feuding with all of your neighbors."

"You think you know hill folk but you don't."

"Enough gabbing," Fargo said. Staying well out of reach, he sidled around in front of Orville. "Get on your horse," he told Belinda while continuing to cover him.

Over at the barn some of the McWhertles were muttering and a few made threatening motions, as if they contemplated rushing over to stop them.

"If they don't behave," Fargo said to Orville, "you'll be the first one I shoot."

Orville looked at them and bellowed, "Quiet down and stay where you are."

Never once taking his pistol off Orville, Fargo climbed on the Ovaro. His boots in the stirrups, the reins in his other hand, he wheeled the stallion and said over his shoulder, "This can end here if you let it."

"Go to hell."

They galloped through the orchard to the road and for another quarter of a mile before Fargo was certain no one was after them. He slowed to a walk and Belinda followed his example.

"I wish we could have prevailed on them to let me stay," she remarked. "Edna needs constant watching."

"Shouldn't you be worrying about something else?" Fargo said.

"The McWhertles? They've threatened me before. All it is, is talk."

"I'm talking about Sawyer and Abigail. What if you're wrong and it *is* rabies?"

"Then heaven help us."

They passed no one on the road. When the lights of Ketchum Falls twinkled in the far distance, Belinda brought her mount next to his and said, "I've been thinking."

Fargo waited.

"Where do you plan to bed down for the night?"

"I hadn't given it any thought."

"Well, if you want, you're welcome to sleep in my parlor. The settee's not all that comfortable but I can spread blankets on the floor."

"What will the neighbors think?"

"I'm a grown woman. I can do as I please. And it's not as if I have a man over every night. In fact, you'll be the first man I've had over since I came here."

"I was joking," Fargo said.

"Oh."

The lights grew brighter and buildings took shape. They were almost to the edge of town when Belinda said, "That's strange. Where is everyone?"

The main street was empty. There wasn't a soul in sight. Nor, Fargo noticed, were there any horses at any of the hitch rails. He drew rein and motioned for her to stop. "Listen," he said.

"I don't hear anything."

"That's just it."

Ketchum Falls didn't have saloons and bawdy houses like a lot of wild and woolly towns west of the Mississippi. But there should have been *some* signs of life and the sounds that went with it.

There should have been voices. There should have been occasional laughter. There should have been the squeals of children.

"Why, the place looks to be practically deserted," Belinda said.

Fargo put his hand on his Colt and clucked to the Ovaro. He stayed in the middle of the street and probed the recesses and doorways.

"Where can everyone have gotten to?" Belinda wondered.

"Look," Fargo said, and nodded at the second floor window of a house. Faces were peering out of them, those of two small children and their mother. All three commenced to frantically wave their arms and point down the street.

"What are they trying to tell us?" Belinda said.

Fargo noticed other faces at other windows, and then he noticed a body. The legs stuck out from the corner of a building. The rest was in a pool of shadow. He reined the Ovaro over.

"Why, it's Marshal Gruel!" Belinda blurted.

Before Fargo could stop her, she swung down and sank to a knee.

"Look at his neck!"

Fargo had already seen; a fist-sized hole in the lawman's throat. He climbed off and touched her shoulder. "We have to hunt cover."

"It can't be," she said. "Not here."

From out of the blackness down the street came a hiss.

# 16

Fargo whirled, his Colt out and up. The skin at the nape of his neck prickled as something took shape in the darkness a couple of blocks down. He heard the scrape of shambling feet, and into the light from a window lurched a man.

The figure was hunched over. The head was turned down. Fargo couldn't see much of the face except for the foam dripping from the chin.

"Oh God. It is," Belinda breathed. "It's another one."

The figured looked up.

"Not him!" she exclaimed.

"I'll be damned," Fargo said.

It was Robin Hood or Dastardly Jack or whatever Timmy Wilson had been calling himself. Timmy shuffled along with his fingers splayed like claws. He looked behind him and then up the street in their direction.

"I hope he doesn't see us," Belinda whispered.

Fargo doubted the boy could. They were in deep shadow. Their horses, though, weren't, as he realized when Timmy Wilson stiffened and stared at the Ovaro and the bay like a wolf ravenous for food.

"Surely not," Belinda said.

Timmy hissed and started toward their mounts.

"He's going to attack our horses," Belinda stated the obvious. "Why would he do that?"

Fargo would have asked her if she'd forgotten about the chickens and the hog and the mule out at Old Man Sawyer's but he had a more pressing concern. Striding past the Ovaro, he extended his arm and yelled, "Stop where you are, boy."

Timmy caterwauled like a mountain cat and broke into a lope. Foam wreathed his mouth and glistened on his neck.

"Don't shoot him," Belinda cried. "He doesn't know what he's doing."

The boy's face split in a fierce, maniacal grin.

Fargo cocked his Colt.

"Please, no," Belinda said. "We must subdue him so I can treat him."

"He bites us, we might come down with it too," Fargo said. The boy was thirty feet away and swiftly closing.

"If it's contagious," Belinda said. "Besides, you've already been bitten on your knuckle."

"Don't remind me," Fargo said, and shot him.

The slug caught Timmy Wilson high in the left thigh and knocked his leg out from under him. Timmy did an ungainly somersault and crashed onto his shoulder. He didn't seem to feel the pain. He pushed onto hands and knees and then shoved upright and limped toward them, his red eyes gleaming with bloodlust.

"Let me try something," Belinda said, and darted past Fargo.

"Get out of the way!" Fargo shouted.

Holding her hands out, Belinda cried, "Stop, Timmy. I beg you. Or he'll shoot you again."

To Fargo's surprise, the boy did stop. Wilson grunted and his brow furrowed and he looked at Belinda as if he was trying to remember something.

"That's it. You know me," Belinda said. "We're friends, you and I. I stood up for you when everyone wanted to punish you over that calf incident. Don't you remember?"

Timmy cocked his head.

"We're friends," Belinda said again. "And if you'll let me examine you, I'm confident I can find a cure for whatever has done this to you."

Timmy snarled.

"Do you have any idea how you contracted the disease? Did someone or something bite you?"

Timmy Wilson crouched.

"Listen to me, Tim. Sort out my words in your head so they make sense. You're not an animal. You're a human being. Do you hear me? You can fight this through force of will. I know you can."

Baring his teeth, Timmy charged her.

Fargo squeezed the trigger.

At the blast Timmy's head erupted in an explosive spray. Timmy

90

took one more stride, and his legs folded under him. He pitched headlong to the ground, hitting hard. His body broke into convulsions. With a last hiss of air escaping from his lungs, he went limp.

"Did you have to?" Belinda sadly asked.

"He was almost on you."

"But did you really have to?"

Fargo commenced replacing the spent cartridges. He heard doors open and subdued voices and footsteps as people came out of buildings up and down the street.

"Is he really dead?" a townsman yelled.

"Dead as hell," Fargo answered.

The townsfolk converged, some of them nervous, some of them fearful, mothers averting the faces of their children.

A man in a suit and bowler stood over Timmy's body and said, "We thank you, mister. He had this whole town terrorized."

"One boy," Fargo said.

"He showed up about two hours ago," another man said. "Just came out of the woods and commenced hissin' at folks. He attacked Meg Tilly's dog and killed it with his bare teeth."

"That's when everyone ran indoors," a woman took up the account when the man stopped. "None of us wanted to be bit."

"Marshal Gruel tried to take Tim into custody," the first man said, and gestured at the lawman's bulk. "That's when this happened."

"That was over an hour ago," a third man said. "We've been hidin' and waitin' for him to leave since."

"One boy," Fargo said again.

"I know what you're thinkin', mister. We should have dealt with him. We should have shot him ourselves. But most of us knew that boy a good long while and we weren't about to shoot one of our own without damn good cause."

"His killing Gruel wasn't enough?"

"Go to hell, mister. You're an outsider. You wouldn't understand."

"We're not yellow, if that's what you're thinkin'."

"Your words," Fargo said.

Several of the men glared and one rubbed the knuckles of his right fist against his left palm. Whatever they were contemplating, Belinda put an end to it by saying, "I need to examine these bodies. I mind find a clue as to what caused Timmy's condition. Will some of you help carry them to my place? I'd be grateful."

No one objected. They were eager to get the bodies off the

street. A lot of people trailed along, talking quietly and gazing apprehensively into the darkness. They were worried there were others out there like Timmy.

Fargo brought the horses. Instead of tying them out front, he took them around to the backyard, which was bordered by a picket fence. He brought both into the yard and closed the gate.

Belinda converted her parlor into an examination room. She had several men carry the kitchen table in. The bodies were laid out side by side and she shooed everyone out so she could set to work.

Fargo asked if there was anything he could do and she replied that he might as well take it easy. He put coffee on to brew, moved a chair close to a window that looked out on the backyard and the horses, and sat with his boots propped on the sill and stared into the night until the coffee was ready. He took a cup to the parlor.

Belinda had gloves on. Her bag was open and instruments had been laid out in a row. She'd stripped Timmy Wilson to the waist and had used a scalpel to open him from sternum to navel. At the moment she was poking around in his organs.

"Do you want some?" Fargo asked, holding out the cup.

"Eh?" Belinda looked up. "No. Thank you. I'm too busy. Leave it, though."

"Found anything?" Fargo asked.

"Not yet. I think I'm going to cut open his stomach and maybe his intestines to see if I can learn what he's eaten recently."

"Have fun," Fargo said, and returned to the kitchen. He poured a cup for himself and sat in the chair and sipped. It had been a rough couple of days and he was beat but he held off going to bed.

The minutes crawled into an hour and the hour into four.

His eyelids were heavy when shoes scraped and Belinda came in. She still wore the gloves, which were covered with gore and blood, and went to the sink.

"Any luck?"

"I'm not sure. I'd have to cut open Old Man Sawyer and Abigail to try and find a common denominator." She stripped off a glove and dropped it in the sink and pried at the other.

"How are you feeling?"

"Fine as can be," Fargo said.

"No fever? No queasiness? No headache? Nothing like that?"

"I'm fine," Fargo said.

"It may well be that bites don't spread the contagion, after all.

Or maybe it's that you were bitten on the knuckle and the disease didn't get into your blood." She pried off the second glove and dropped it, then turned and leaned against the counter. A portrait of weariness, she swiped at a bang and said, "I must look a mess."

"You're the sexiest sawbones ever," Fargo said.

Belinda smiled. "Why is it men think of one thing and one thing only?"

"You answered your own question."

Laughing, Belinda went to a cupboard. "I needed that to help me take my mind off the gruesomeness of it all. I've never enjoyed cutting people open but there are times when it has to be done."

"They were past caring what you did," Fargo said.

"And I don't want others to share their fate." She took down a cup and saucer. "Perhaps I should contact the governor and have him impose a quarantine."

"How would you get word to him?"

"I'd have to ride there myself, I suppose." Belinda stepped to the stove and picked up the pot. "He'd need to hear it from my lips."

"Nice lips," Fargo said.

"Have you been thinking of that the whole while you've been waiting?"

"That and other things."

"Such as?"

"I should go after Old Man Sawyer in the morning. He's still running around out there, foaming at the mouth."

"You would do that? After how you've been treated?"

Fargo regarded his knuckle. "I have as much at stake as anyone in finding out what this is." He touched the tiny bite mark. "You could say I have more."

"If you find him it would be wonderful if you could take him alive and bring him here for me to examine."

"Taking Abigail alive was hard enough."

"I know. I ask a lot." Belinda sipped and came over and placed her hand on his shoulder. "Don't think I don't appreciate your help. If there's ever anything I can do for you, let me know what and when."

Fargo ran his gaze from her lips to her bosom to her winsome legs. "There is," he said. "And right now is as good a time as any."

# 17

"You can't be serious."

"Try me."

"I'm a mess," Belinda said, and fussed with her hair. "I'd have to wash up first."

"I'm not going anywhere," Fargo said.

Belinda blushed and glanced down the hall and bit her bottom lip. "Why not?" she said, more to herself than to him. "Give me ten minutes."

"Take as long as you like."

She turned and started out but stopped and looked back at him. "Are you always so easy to get along with?"

"Orville and the rest of his dumb-as-stumps clan don't think so."

"I mean, with women."

"You're wasting time," Fargo said.

Belinda smiled coyly, and with a swirl of her dress, she was gone.

Grinning, Fargo refilled his cup. If he knew anything at all about females, she'd take a lot more than ten minutes. He went down the hall to the parlor. She'd draped sheets over the bodies. In a bucket by the table were organs she had removed.

The bucket was speckled with blood and small pieces of whatever she had dropped in it.

Fargo continued on to the front door. She'd forgotten to throw the bolt. He opened it and stepped out for some fresh air.

Ketchum Falls lay quiet under the stars. Not many lights were on at that hour. He scanned the street but saw no one out and about. Somewhere off in the forest a fox yelped.

Going back in, Fargo threw the bolt. He made a circuit of the rooms, checking that the windows were latched. Returning to the kitchen, he opened the back door to check on the Ovaro. It was dozing. He closed the door and worked the bolt.

Draining the cup, Fargo placed it on the counter. He didn't care to sit in the parlor with the bodies so he stayed in the kitchen, in the chair by the window, until nearly an hour later when a soft rustle made him look around. The wait had been worth it.

Belinda was enough to make any man hungry with desire.

She'd not only washed up, she'd done her hair, too, and it cascaded in a bright sheen past her slender shoulders. Instead of the ankle-length dress, she had on a sheer white nightdress that left little to the imagination. It wasn't see-through but it might as well be. He could see her nipples outlined against the white, like hard tacks. And at the junction of her thighs was a darker triangle. He felt a lump in his throat, and swallowed.

"Do you like it?" she shyly asked.

"Never liked anything more," Fargo said.

Belinda plucked at the fabric. "It's the only one like this I own. I hardly ever wear it."

Fargo rose and walked over and placed his hands on her hips.

"You'll be gentle, won't you?" she asked, looking into his eyes.

"I left my whip and chains in Denver."

Belinda laughed. "I'm serious. I don't have a lot of experience at this."

"It will come naturally," Fargo said, and kissed her lightly on the lips.

"I hope so. I don't mind admitting how nervous I am. I'm afraid you won't like me."

"What's not to like?" Fargo rejoined, and switched his hands from her hips to her breasts.

At the contact Belinda gasped and stiffened. Her red lips parted in an oval. "Oh! You get right to it."

Fargo squeezed. She moaned and closed her eyes. He fused his mouth to hers and tasted mint on her breath. Her lips parted and he touched his tongue to hers in a wet dance. Belinda forgot her inhibitions and ground her nether mound against his rigid pole.

"Goodness," she gasped when they broke for breath. "You make my head spin."

"I'll do more than that," Fargo said, cupping her rounded, firm bottom.

"Shouldn't we go up to my bedroom?" she suggested. "We'd be much more comfortable on my bed."

"We'll get there," Fargo said. Pressing her against the wall, he ran his hands over her breasts and down over her belly to her legs even as he ran his mouth over her throat and her ears.

Belinda uttered another moan.

Fargo caressed from her hip to her knees and up again. He pressed the tips of two fingers to the bottom tip of the dark triangle, and she shuddered.

"Mercy me," Belinda breathed. "You better get me to bed. My legs are so weak, I don't know as I can stand."

Tucking, Fargo scooped her into his arms. He went on kissing her as he carried her down the hall and up the curved flight of stairs. Her bedroom door was wide open. Her bed was a surprise: a four-poster with a rose-colored canopy. She had already folded the quilt at the bottom and drawn a pink blanket back. Two long pillows and two small ones were arranged along the top.

"Be gentle," Belinda said again as he set her down.

Fargo unbuckled his gun belt and set it on her dresser. Sitting on the bed, he removed his spurs and let them drop. He tugged out of his boots. Finally he stretched out next to her and reignited her spark by kissing her long and hard.

"What you do to me," she cooed when the kiss ended. "You positively make my heart flutter."

"Less talk," Fargo said.

"I'm sorry," Belinda said. "I told you I was nervous and when I'm nervous I tend to gab."

"Put your mouth to better use."

"As you wish, handsome," Belinda said demurely, and applied her wet lips to his throat. Her hands were on his chest.

Fargo hiked at her night dress and got it as high as her knees. He delved under and roamed his palm along her satiny skin, ever higher until he slid his hand between her legs. Belinda sucked in a breath and bowed her forehead to his chin.

He ran a finger along her moist slit and she shivered. He parted her nether lips and her whole body shook. He circled her tiny knob with his fingertip and she suddenly gripped him and pumped her hips and cried out.

Just like that, she gushed.

Fargo had barely begun. He kissed her as she thrashed and moaned.

"My heavens," she whispered when she subsided. "This will be a night I'll never forget."

Fargo hiked her dress above her waist and up over her twin globes. Her mounds were like ripe melons. He nipped a nipple with his teeth and she arched. He pinched the other nipple and she glued her hot mouth to his as if seeking to devour him.

For a long while they kissed and fondled. She ran her hands all over him but only above his waist. To encourage her to delve lower, he took her hand and placed it on his bulge.

"Oh!" Belinda exclaimed. "You're so big."

"Rub it," Fargo said huskily.

"You really want me to?"

Of all the stupid questions Fargo had ever been asked, that took the cake. He moved her hand up and down and she took the hint and commenced moving it herself.

"Like that?"

Fargo grunted. The sensations she provoked made it hard not to explode.

"How about this?" Belinda said, and squeezed him.

The lump was back in Fargo's throat.

"Or this?" Belinda said, and gently closed her fingers on the tip. Now it was Fargo who arched his back.

"You do like that, don't you?"

"Shut the hell up and fuck me." Fargo pulled her to him and covered her mouth with his. He squeezed and massaged her breasts until she panted with need. Lower down, he rubbed and stroked. Her legs parted and he inserted a finger into her sheath. For a moment she was perfectly still. He stroked and her bottom came off the bed. When he inserted a second finger, she gripped both his shoulders and dug her nails in so deep, it hurt.

"Please," she said.

Fargo went on stroking. She shook and pulled at his hair and her eyes fluttered and she gushed a second time, more violently than the first. Afterward, she clung to him, taking deep breaths and mewing deep in her throat.

"I didn't know it could be like this," she whispered. "It's heaven."

Fargo spread her legs wider and eased onto his knees between them. He held his pole and rubbed it along her slit and her face flushed with lust.

"Yes. Do it. Put it in me."

He didn't need encouragement. Penetrating only an inch or so, he smiled at her and suddenly rammed in to the hilt. She voiced an inarticulate peal of pleasure and drove against him as if to batter him senseless. He plunged, pulled back, plunged again.

Under them the four-poster moved as if to an earthquake.

Fargo took his time. He let the inevitable build until there was no holding back, not for her, and certainly not for him. The room seemed to burst at the seams and she drenched him with her release. They pumped and pumped and eventually coasted to a mutual stop with her gasping and his chest pounding. Cushioned by her softness, he lay on top of her and caught his breath.

"You're magnificent," Belinda breathed.

"Don't spoil it," Fargo said.

"How does my complimenting you spoil things?"

"Just don't."

Fargo rolled off her and lay on his side. Sleep tugged at him and he let himself drift off. How long he was out he couldn't say but when his eyes snapped open he was cold, his skin covered with goose bumps. He raised his head, wondering what woke him.

Belinda was sound asleep, her bare breasts rising and falling to the rhythm of her breathing. Every now and then she let out a soft snore.

Fargo lowered his cheek to the bed. He could use more sleep. But no sooner did he close his eyes than he heard a noise from the rear of the house. He raised his head again, trying to identify it. It might have been the thud of a hoof.

Recalling the dead mule out at Old Man Sawyer's, he sat up. He tried to tell himself that the odds of the old lunatic coming to town and attacking the Ovaro were slim. But Robin Hood Timmy had shown up there and had gone after the stallion and Belinda's horse.

Better safe than lose the best horse he'd ever known, Fargo decided. Sliding off the bed, he pulled his pants up and pulled on his boots. He left his spurs on the floor. Rather than take the time to strap on his gun belt, he snatched the Colt from its holster and hurried down. As he went past the parlor he noticed the clock on the mantle. It was almost four thirty.

Fargo moved along the hall to the kitchen. He slid the bolt and opened the door and stepped out into the chill air. He needn't have worried. The Ovaro and the doc's horse were over by the picket fence. Neither was asleep. Their heads were up and they were looking in his direction. He thought they were staring at him until a gun muzzle was jammed against his temple.

"One twitch," Abner McWhertle said, "and I'll by God blow your brains out."

# 18

The night disgorged more than a dozen of them. Clyde was there, his shoulder bandaged, and other faces Fargo recognized from the farm.

Orville towered above the rest. He came up and gripped the Colt, careful not to stand in front of the muzzle. "I'll take that."

With Abner's revolver to his temple, Fargo didn't have any choice. He frowned and let go. "What the hell are you jackasses up to?"

"We're doin' what we told you we would do," Abner gleefully crowed.

"You better not," Fargo said.

"We're scared, mister," Clyde taunted. "We're real scared."

Some of the men laughed.

Orville wedged Fargo's Colt under his belt and half turned. "All right, Mabel. You and the others can get to it."

To Fargo's surprise, Orville's wife and eight other women came out of concealment. Mabel marched up to him and glared.

"You hit me, mister."

"You deserved it, bitch."

"Did I, now?" Mabel retorted, and kicked him in the shin.

Fargo nearly buckled. The pain shot clear through him. Gritting his teeth, he stayed on his feet.

"None of that, woman," Orville said. "And don't be beatin' on her, either."

"Her?" Fargo said.

"Who do you think?" Orville said, and opened the back door.

Mabel and the other women quietly filed in.

"Damn it, Orville," Fargo said. "All she did was try to help you."

"We didn't want her help," Orville said. "We made that plain as plain could be. She should have listened."

"That she should have," said a new voice, and out of the dark strolled Charles T. Dogood, his hands thrust in his pockets.

"This is your doing," Fargo said.

Dogood smiled. "I might have persuaded them that having her around does me no favors. And I do, after all, have their best interests at heart."

Fargo looked at Orville. "Don't do this."

"It's already been decided." Orville snapped his fingers and more of his clan appeared. They were carrying two rails and a bucket that reeked of sulfurous fumes.

"You son of a bitch," Fargo said.

Orville punched him in the gut.

Fargo's stomach exploded and he doubled over. He almost collapsed.

Abner and Clyde laughed. "Serves you right, mister," the former said. "The airs you put on."

Orville wrapped a huge hand around Fargo's throat and bent so they were eye to eye. "I'd be real careful what I say from here on out if I were you. I've put up with a lot, mister, but it ends, here and now. We are doin' it and that is all there is to it." He shoved Fargo against the wall. "It will be up to you whether we do it easy or hard."

Fargo fought the pain and said through clenched teeth, "You do this, you step over a line."

"What line are you talkin' about?"

"No return."

Abner snorted. "What in hell is he talkin' about, cousin? I don't see no line."

"It's there," Fargo said.

"He's trying to confuse you, gentlemen," Dogood said. "Stick to your guns."

"Speakin' of which," Orville said to Clyde, and handed Fargo's Colt over to him. "Tie him good and tight."

Several men came forward, one with a rope.

"Like hell," Fargo said. He unleashed an uppercut that sent the man with the rope toppling. Spinning, he drove his fist into a jaw, shifted, and clipped another McWhertle on the cheek. An opening appeared and he tried to dart through it but a foot hooked his leg and he tripped and came down on his hands and knees. Immediately, four of them were on him, seeking to pin him. He fought in a fury. He bucked. He punched. He kicked. They hit him but he didn't care. He connected with a nose and the weight was off him. Pushing to his feet, he took a step toward the Ovaro but they were on him again, more of them, seven or eight, and he went down under their crushing numbers.

He was stripped to the waist and his arms were wrenched behind his back and his wrists were bound tight. His ankles were bound, too. A gag was forced into his mouth and he bit at the fingers. A blow to his jaw dazed him enough that they were able to shove the gag in, but he spat it back out.

They stepped back, some of them bleeding, two of them limping.

"Hellfire, he fights like a wildcat," one said.

"I'd surely love to stomp his brains out," said another.

Orville came over. "We're not a bunch of red savages. We do this proper. And we do it quick and quiet so no one hears us. Remember, she has friends."

At the word "she," the screen door opened and out came the women. Mabel had hold of Belinda Jackson. They had tied her wrists.

"Can you believe it?" Mabel said to Orville. "She didn't resist. Just kept askin' us to come to our senses and see that this is wrong."

"It is," Belinda said quietly.

"Puny cow," Abner mocked her.

"Please," Belinda appealed to Orville. "They look up to you. Ultimately, this is on your shoulders. Say the word and they'll go home and I'll forget this ever happened."

"Listen to her," Clyde said, and chortled.

"We warned you," Orville said.

"And what about Harold and Edna and Abigail? I might be able to treat them, I tell you."

Mabel's mouth twisted in scorn. "No need, missy. We took care of that our own selves."

"How?"

"How do you think?" Mabel said.

Belinda stared at their faces. Her own slowly registered disbelief and then horror. "You didn't," she gasped.

Orville nodded. "We couldn't have them goin' around bitin' folks so we put them out of their misery."

"You *killed* them?"

Orville nodded again. "We were humane about it. We shot Harold in the back of the head while he was sleepin'. Edna didn't ever come around and was hardly breathin' so it was nothin' to smother her with a pillow."

"And Abigail?" Belinda said.

"I took care of her," Mabel said. "Stuck her head in a bucket of water and drowned her like I would kittens we didn't want." She chuckled. "That girl sure kicked up a fuss but it was over pretty quick."

"Oh God," Belinda said.

"Enough of her mewin'," Mabel said angrily. "Someone gag this bitch so we can get to it."

"That we better," Orville said, gazing along the backs of the houses. "There shouldn't be anyone out and about at this hour but you never know."

Belinda looked about her in shock. "What kind of people are you that you can do these things?"

"Don't you lecture us," Mabel said. "We do what we have to to protect our own. Always have. Always will." She slapped Belinda, not once but three times.

Belinda stood there and let her. Tears formed at the corners of her eyes and trickled down her cheeks.

"Look at her," Abner said in disgust.

"Figures," Clyde said. "That's city folks for you."

They grabbed Belinda and lowered her to the ground and held her while Mabel tied her ankles.

"Bring the rails," Orville commanded.

Two men brought one each and laid them out next to Fargo and Belinda.

"Let me do the bitch," Mabel said. Squatting, she slammed Belinda's wrists against the rail and began to tie her to it.

"No need to be so rough," Orville remarked.

"Sure there is," Mabel said. "Her always treatin' us like we were ignorant. Well, this will show the bitch." She slapped Belinda across the face. "We want her to get it through her thick head that she's not wanted here, don't we? Nothin' like a little hurt to convince a person."

"I agree," Abner said. Without warning, he stepped up to Fargo and kicked him in the ribs.

Another explosion of pain nearly blacked Fargo out. Sucking in air through his nose, he waited for the waves of agony to subside.

"Enough of that, I say," Orville said. "Other folks hereabouts won't raise a fuss about us runnin' these two out. But if we hurt them, they will."

"What do we care?" Mabel said.

"We live here. We have to get along with them best we can. No more smackin' and kickin'."

"Aw, hell," Abner said. "I was just gettin' started."

Fargo was barely aware of being tied to the rail. He struggled to regain his senses. They cleared just as two brawny men laid hands on both ends of the rail and jerked it into the air. His body sagged, compliments of gravity, his shoulders protesting the strain.

Belinda was being similarly raised.

Clyde giggled. "They sort of remind me of hogs trussed for slaughter."

Dogood materialized at Fargo's shoulder. "I do so hope there won't be any hard feelings. After all, you brought this on yourself."

"Bring the tar," Orville commanded.

The reeking bucket was placed on the ground under Fargo.

Orville was handed a ladle used for stew and the like. He dipped it and stirred. "We heated it good and proper before we came but it's cooled some."

"Should we heat it again?" Abner asked. "The hotter it is, the more misery they'll be in."

"No time," Orville said. "It will be light in an hour or so. We'll do it as is."

"You are no fun sometimes, cousin," Abner said.

Orville raised the ladle and tilted it and black sludge dripped over the rim.

All Fargo could do was glare. A warm sensation spread across his chest and over his stomach as the gooey tar slowly spread. The stink made him crinkle his nose.

Mabel was doing the same to Belinda, and commented, "I still say we should have stripped her."

"It wouldn't be decent," Orville said.

"But it's not the same, tarrin' and featherin' her nightdress."

"She won't ever get the tar out," Orville said. "She'll never be able to wear it again."

"That's no kind of punishment. She deserves worse."

"While I tend to agree," Charlie Dogood interjected, "I suppose your husband has a point, my dear. We should be civil about this."

The tar covered Fargo's shoulders. There was some on his hips and legs.

"This is fun," Mabel said, upending her ladle over Belinda's head.

Orville bent and dipped the ladle in the bucket and held it over Fargo's. "I hear tell you'll have to cut your hair plumb off."

Clyde did more giggling.

"You're right, Mabel," Orville said. "This is kind of fun." And he started to turn the ladle.

# 19

The slam of a back door down the street caused the McWhertles to glance up.

"What the dickens is goin' on over there?" a man shouted. "Folks are tryin' to sleep and all we hear is your jabber."

"Mind your own business," Abner hollered.

The man wasn't intimidated. "How about I fetch my shotgun and come mind yours?"

"I'd like to see you try," Abner said.

"Hush up," Orville told him, "or you'll wake half the town."

As if to prove him right, a window on a house across the way slid open and a woman's head poked out. "What in tarnation is all the ruckus about over there? Who are you people and what are you doin' at Doc Jackson's?"

Abner went to yell but Orville wagged the ladle at him and said, "When I tell you to hush, you damn well better hush."

To the woman he replied, "One of our kin is sick, ma'am. The doc is tendin' to him."

The man down the street yelled, "Well keep it down, damn you. People are tryin' to sleep."

The back door slammed and the window across the way slid down and the night was quiet again.

"Let's finish with the tar and tote them off like we were fixin' to do," Clyde said.

"No," Orville said. He put the ladle in the bucket and handed the bucket to another McWhertle. "We're leavin' this minute. Get the horses."

"But why?" Abner protested. "They ain't hardly covered with goo."

Orville gestured at the houses. "You heard those two. We might

*106*

have woke others and some yak will take it into his head to come for a look-see. We don't want the whole town turnin' out against us."

"Hell," a scruffy cousin said. "We can lick 'em."

Mabel rose. "I am disappointed in you, husband. I thought you had more gumption."

"You want to see gumption?" Orville said. Taking a stride, he cuffed her across the face, a backhand that sent her tottering. She lost her grip on her ladle and it clattered to the ground. "Mouth off to me again in front of our kin and I'll bust you good."

Mabel had a hand to her cheek and was struggling to control her temper.

"I can't hear you," Orville said.

"Sorry," Mabel spat. "It won't happen again."

"It sure as hell better not." Orville rounded on the others. "Anyone else want to give me lip?"

No one spoke.

"I want the horses. I want the horses now. Move your asses, by God."

They scrambled to obey.

Fargo looked at Belinda. Tar covered half her hair and had dripped down the left side of her face. Only her right eye, her nose and cheek and her mouth were free of it. Her nightdress a mess. "How are you holding up?"

Her eye glistened. "All I ever wanted to do was help them."

"No talkin', you two," Abner growled.

Fargo stared at him.

"Why are you lookin' at me like that?"

Fargo went on staring.

"Stop it, you hear?" Abner said, shifting his weight from one foot to the other. "It's like you've givin' me the evil eye or somethin'."

"Or something," Fargo said.

The horses were brought and everyone quietly mounted except for the four men picked to carry the rails. One by one the clan filed out the gate and down the side street and, by a roundabout route of more side streets, soon reached the edge of Ketchum Falls.

In the wee hour before dawn the town was as still as a cemetery. No one was out and about. No one demanded to know who they were and what they were up to.

Fargo swayed with every step his bearers took. His shoulders became sore as hell.

A horse swung in alongside the rail he was tied to, and who should be in the saddle but Charles T. Dogood. He smirked and said, "It's a shame we were interrupted. I once saw a man covered with tar from head to toe. They had to peel it off him after it dried. Took off most of his skin, too."

"You brought this on them," Fargo said.

Dogood glanced down sharply. "Brought what, friend? I'm not sure I understand."

"One thing we'll never be," Fargo said, "is friends."

"What did I bring?" Dogood demanded.

"You brought them to this," Fargo answered, with a nod at the rail.

"Oh. That." The patent medicine man grinned. "It wasn't entirely my doing. They are a proud people, the McWhertles. They stand up for one another."

"Tell that to Harold and Edna and the little girl."

"Orville did what needed doing. Just as he needed to tar and feather the good doctor. He's tried for years to convince her to hang her shingle somewhere else but she was too stubborn for her own good."

"There's a lot of that going around," Fargo said.

"Meaning me, I suppose?"

"With you it's not stubbornness," Fargo said. "With you it's that you're snake-mean."

"I am no such thing," Dogood said indignantly. "Ask anyone and they will tell you I'm the kindest person they know."

"You pretend to be. You smile and you flatter them and they can't see the oil for the teeth."

"You're suggesting I have a shady character?"

"There's no suggest about it."

Dogood bent down. "Do you know what? I'm glad they did this. You deserve to be put in your place. You're entirely too sure of yourself." He sniffed and gigged his horse.

Belinda must have been listening because she said, "I never truly realized how petty that man is."

"He's worse than petty," Fargo said.

"Shut up, both of you," one of the men carrying him snapped. "You don't talk unless we say."

They had gone about a quarter of a mile when Orville called for them to halt. Dismounting, he motioned for the rails to be set on the ground.

The pair lowering Fargo's let it drop from waist-high. Wincing, he made it a point to memorize their faces.

Orville went to Belinda. "Have we gotten it through that noggin of yours?"

"This was wrong, Orville McWhertle. I'll never forgive you for mistreating me so."

"It's for your own good," Orville said.

"Oh, that's a good one," Belinda said. "Next you'll be assuring me the tar is good for my complexion."

"Damn it, woman. You ain't got no sense. Consider this your last warnin'. Your very last. We tried reasonin' with you and it didn't work. We talked ourselves blue in the face makin' it clear we don't want you here but you stayed on anyway."

Mabel had come up. "You tell her, Orville. Tell the bitch how it is."

"You poor, misguided souls," Belinda said.

"How dare you look down your nose at us," Mabel said, and before anyone could guess her intent, she kicked Belinda in the chest. Belinda cried out and Mabel drew her leg back to kick her again.

"Enough of that," Orville said.

Mabel clearly yearned to go on kicking. She glared at him and then at Belinda. "You're lucky he's so softhearted or I'd stomp you silly."

Orville hunkered and waited until Belinda stopped quaking and gasping. "Take your city ways and your city doctorin' and go somewhere folks will cotton to you. You're not wanted here. You're not welcome here. Charlie Dogood is our healer. We don't need no one else."

"Thank you, friend Orville," Dogood said.

"What about him?" Abner asked, with a bob of his chin at Fargo. "Could be he might take it into his head to come after us."

"Maybe we should break his legs," Clyde suggested. "He can't come after us if he can't walk nor ride."

Orville switched his attention to Fargo. "Good point, cousins. What about you, mister? Are you goin' to leave this be?"

"Would you?" Fargo said.

"I knew it," Abner spat.

"Bust his legs and some of his fingers, besides," Clyde urged.

"Did you hear them?" Orville said. "I want your word that you'll get on that horse of yours and light a shuck."

"What makes you think he'd keep it?" Abner asked.

"This one would," Orville said. "If you were a better judge of character, you'd know." To Fargo he said, "I'll ask you again, for the last time. Give me your word."

"Can't," Fargo said.

"You're makin' this awful hard on yourself."

"I told you about the line."

"Be reasonable, damn it."

Fargo looked at the tar on his chest and pants and over at Belinda and back at Orville. "That's damn funny coming from you."

Orville sighed and unfurled. "You know, boys. I reckon you have a point. This jasper is too thickheaded."

"Do we get to break his legs?" Clyde eagerly asked.

"You get to kick and beat on him some," Orville said. "Enough to convince him to go, which he can't do with broke legs."

"That'll have to do, I guess," Clyde said, sounding disappointed.

"This will add to it," Fargo said to Orville.

"There's no talkin' to you." Orville motioned. "Show him what we think of someone who's so goddamn stupid, boys."

Fargo tried to protect himself. He brought his legs as far toward his chest as they would go and hunched his shoulders to offer less of his neck and head for their blows. Four of them pounced, Abner and Clyde and two others. Laughing and grinning, they rained punches and kicks on his chest, legs and arms. The pain was excruciating. In their excitement they jostled one another. A kick Abner aimed at his shoulder struck his cheek and bright spots of light pinwheeled before his eyes.

"That's enough," Orville said.

All of them stopped except Abner. He went on kicking and grinning.

"I said that's enough," Orville repeated himself.

Reluctantly, Abner stepped back.

"How badly are you hurt?" Belinda asked.

Fargo couldn't answer. It was all he could do not to groan; he'd be damned if he'd give them the satisfaction.

"Someone hand me a knife," Orville said, and when one was shoved into his hand, he bent down. "Time to end this."

# 20

The blade flashed in the starlight. The rope that bound Fargo's wrists to the rail gave way as Orville cut the Trailsman free.

"What did you do that for?" Abner asked.

"We should leave them trussed," Clyde declared.

"You are too softhearted, husband," Mabel complained.

Orville ignored them. "You can do the rest yourself, and her," he said to Fargo. He climbed on his horse and reined toward town. "If you're smart you'll fan the breeze. Collect your horse and your effects and go. We catch you hangin' around, there will be blood." He clucked to his animal and the McWhertles rode off in a body into the night.

As Abner went by he glanced down and laughed.

Mabel deliberately passed so close to Belinda that her horse nearly trod on her.

The rumble of their hooves faded and the only sound was the wind and Belinda's soft sobs.

Fargo was a welter of pain. His arms, his legs, his sides. He hurt over every square inch. But he could endure the pain.

He'd been beaten on before. Worse than this, in fact. It was the other thing that rankled. It was the other thing that he couldn't live with and still call himself a man.

Sitting up, he pried at the rope around his ankles. It took a considerable while. It would be easier if he used the toothpick but he couldn't get at the ankle sheath in his boot. The knots were tight and his fingers were stiff and the simple act of moving made him hurt worse. The smell of the tar was getting to him. He plucked off as much as he could before it could dry and wiped his fingers in the grass.

Belinda involuntarily started when he touched her cheek.

"I'll have you free in a minute."

"Oh, Skye," she said, and went on sobbing.

Fargo slid his fingers down his boot and palmed the Arkansas toothpick. A few cuts and the rope lay on the ground. She had so much tar on her that he got some on his hands when he helped her to stand.

"How could they?" She placed her brow to his chest and cried in earnest.

Fargo let her weep. He made a silent vow then and there.

She was a good woman, this Belinda Jackson. But even if she wasn't, even if she'd been the worst bitch to draw breath, she didn't deserve this. When she was reduced to sniffling he touched her elbow.

"We need to get that tar off your face."

"How?" she said. "Hot water and a lot of scraping is about the only thing that will work."

"Let me see what I can do."

Fargo exercised great care. Between his fingernails and a light application of the toothpick in a gentle scraping motion, he got a lot of it off her forehead and her cheek and her chin. She couldn't open her left eye but it was better than it had been. "I can cut off the night-dress," he offered, knowing what she would say.

"And have me walk about in the altogether? No thank you. I have a little dignity left."

They started back. The air was cool and Fargo's chest grew cold but it was the least of his considerations. He kept the toothpick in his right hand, just in case. In that part of the country there were bears and mountain lions—and people who went around foaming at the mouth.

Belinda plodded along with her head bowed. All the vitality seemed to have drained out of her. Halfway to the settlement she cleared her throat.

"Maybe they're right. Maybe I've been too stubborn for my own good."

"Don't let them win," Fargo said.

"Look at me," Belinda said. "Look at what my stubbornness has brought me to."

"You said it yourself. A lot of people in Ketchum Falls like you. A lot don't want you to go anywhere."

"But that's just it. The people who don't won't ever accept me.

low can I live up to my Hippocratic oath if half those I came to elp won't let me touch them?"

"It's them, not you."

"I can't force anyone to accept me. It's been wrong of me to hink I can."

"So you give up and go?"

In the dark it looked as if she shrugged. "There are other towns, ther communities. Places where I'd be accepted. Places where I vouldn't have to fight my own patients."

"You want my advice?" Fargo asked, and didn't wait for her to nswer. "Stay in Ketchum Falls. The people who want you here eserve that. And the clan that did this to you won't ever do it again."

"What are you saying?"

Fargo didn't respond.

"You're going to do as they want and leave, aren't you?"

"No."

"But you heard Orville. They're through being nice."

"So am I."

Belinda went to put her hand on his arm and caught herself and ooked at the tar covering her hand. "Listen to me. Please. I don't vant blood to be spilled."

"Orville said it."

"There will be blood?" Belinda remembered. "But that takes you down to their level."

"Fine by me."

"Please," Belinda said. "I'm not thinking only of them. I'm hinking of you. You're just one man and there are a lot of them."

"An army is only as strong as its general."

"You can't take the law into your own hands."

"There *is* no law in Ketchum Falls. Not with Gruel dead. And there's the other thing, too."

"What other thing?"

"The so-called rabies."

"What are you saying? That you know what it is?"

"Someone said something that gave me a notion," Fargo said. He didn't elaborate.

"You don't care to share it?"

Fargo was spared from having to answer by the clatter and rattle of a wagon coming up behind them. They stopped and waited and shortly a buckboard came around the last bend. In the seat was a burly farmer in overalls, a straw hat on his head. The sky had lightened enough that he saw them right away and smiled and brought his team to a stop. In the bed were half a dozen large milk cans.

"Good morning, Mr. Tilman," Belinda said.

The farmer's mouth fell open in astonishment. He looked from her to Fargo and back again. "What in heaven? Is that you Dr. Jackson?"

"Afraid so," Belinda said.

"Why, you've got tar all over you."

"Afraid so," Belinda said again. "There are supposed to be feathers but they were interrupted before they could get around to that part."

"Who is this *they* you're talkin' about?" Tilman asked, his outrage apparent. "Who did this to you, Doc? Who would dare do such a thing?"

"I'd rather not say."

"You shouldn't protect them."

"I agree," Fargo said.

Belinda motioned at him. "This is my friend. They did the same to him, as you can see. I don't suppose you'd be willing to take us the rest of the way into town and drop us off at my house?"

"I sure as blazes will."

Belinda thanked him for being so kind and they climbed into the bed so as not to get tar all over the seat.

As they were making themselves comfortable the farmer said "Think nothin' of this, Doc. You helped my Maude, remember, that time she had the croup? There's a lot of us who are in your debt."

"I do what I do because I like to help people. No one is obligated to me."

Tilman scowled and made a fist. "I wish you'd tell me who's to blame. I'll round up some others and we'll show them what we think of doin' this to a fine lady like yourself."

"That's exactly what I don't want," Belinda said. "More trouble on my account." She looked pointedly at Fargo.

Tilman sat and got his team moving. "I can't believe it. There hasn't been anyone tarred or feathered in Coogan County in a coon's age. And to do it to you, of all people."

Fargo stayed silent. He had nothing to say, anyway, except to

**114**

thank the farmer when they were let off. Tilman drove off to deliver the milk and Belinda led him around to the back and into the kitchen.

"I don't want to go upstairs like this. I'll get tar all over everything. Would you mind fetching a blanket?"

Fargo had been looking for his Colt. It wasn't there. The McWhertles had taken it. One more thing they had to answer for.

He found a blanket where she said one would be, in a closet upstairs, and brought it down. In the meantime she had removed her nightdress and was digging at the tar on her head.

"This will take forever."

"I'll help," Fargo said.

She wrapped the blanket around her and they spent over an hour wiping and scraping. By now she was mostly free of the worst of it.

Belinda stepped to the stove. "I'll have hot water ready in ten minutes or so. You can wash first if you'd like."

"There's no hurry," Fargo said. The McWhertles weren't going anywhere. He went out to the Ovaro. In his saddlebags was a spare buckskin shirt and pants. He also shucked the Henry from the scabbard.

When he went in, Belinda was crying.

He swore under his breath and put a hand on her shoulder and squeezed. "Don't let them win."

"I'm sorry," she said. "I can't help it."

A large pot of water was on the stove. Fargo set down his spare buckskins and the Henry and tested the water with his finger. It was only lukewarm. He sat in a chair to wait.

Belinda dabbed at the eye that hadn't been covered with tar. "I guess I'm not as strong as I thought I was."

"You've been through hell."

"They didn't really hurt me," Belinda said. "They didn't beat on me like they did on you. And the loss of a nightdress doesn't bother me much."

"Quit making excuses for them."

She studied him. "How can you sit there so calmly? Doesn't it bother you even a little bit?"

"Someone kicks me in the teeth, I get mad," Fargo said. "I don't cry like a baby." He regretted saying that and sought to make amends by adding, "Not that there's anything wrong with a good cry now and then."

"I'm not as strong as you. I thought I was but this has torn me up inside. I can't go on as if nothing happened."

"Me either," Fargo said.

"What will you do to them?"

Fargo stared at the pot. Steam was rising; soon the water would be hot enough.

"I asked you a question."

"I'll do what I have to."

"Be more specific. Give me some idea of what the McWhertles are in store for."

Fargo thought about it and gave her a straight answer.

"They're in for hell on earth."

# 21

Abner McWhertle's farm was four and a half miles south of Ketchum Falls. He owned three hundred acres, nearly all of it tilled. Fields of corn and wheat were ripening under the sun.

Cows grazed in a pasture.

Fargo didn't want to be spotted so he waited until the sun went down. Emerging from a stand of oaks he had hidden in since late afternoon, he climbed on and rode up the lane at a walk. He'd heard barking earlier and he was alert for the dog. When he was within fifty yards of the farmhouse he drew rein and dismounted and continued on foot.

Abner was prosperous. The house and barn were well maintained. There was a chicken coop and a hog pen.

Most of the windows were lit. A lantern was on in the barn, too, and a shadow kept flitting across the open door. Someone was in there.

Fargo crept toward the barn. He came up behind the door, poked his head out for a quick look, and inwardly smiled.

A dozen dairy cows were along one side. Abner was going along the line, forking hay.

Fargo moved around the door and leveled the Henry.

Abner's back was to him and Abner was humming. He turned and saw him and blurted, "You!"

"Miss me?" Fargo asked.

Abner took a step and raised the pitchfork as if to hurl it but stopped and gauged the ten or so feet between them and lowered it again.

"I wish you'd try," Fargo said.

"What are you here for?" Abner demanded. "And how did you know where I live, anyhow?"

"A little bird told me," Fargo said. "As for why I'm here, you can't be *that* stupid."

"You go to hell."

"You first," Fargo taunted.

Abner gazed out the door toward the farmhouse. "Damn it all. My gun is inside. I don't usually carry it when I'm doin' my chores."

"Too bad," Fargo said.

"You won't up and shoot me in cold blood, will you?" Abner said. There was fear in his voice.

Fargo had no intention of killing him. Beating him senseless, that was something else. "Give me one good reason why I shouldn't."

"I have your six-shooter."

Fargo was hoping he did. It was why he'd picked Abner's place first. "Where?"

"In the house. Let me fetch it. And if I give it back, we're even."

"Not hardly," Fargo said. He moved aside and motioned with the Henry. "Walk in front of me and keep your hands where I can see them."

Abner nodded and took a step.

"Drop the damn pitchfork."

"Oh. Sorry." Abner frowned and let it fall. "I forgot I was holdin' it."

"Like hell you did." Fargo didn't trust the man as far as he could throw the barn. He stayed several feet behind as they went out. Lilac bushes decorated the yard and as they passed one a large four-legged shape appeared out of the darkness behind it, and growled.

Instantly, Abner pointed at Fargo and screeched, "Get him, boy! Kill! Kill!"

It happened so fast that Fargo barely had time to jerk the Henry to his shoulder. Before he could shoot the dog was on him. It leaped at his throat and he slammed the barrel against its head, knocking it down. In the bat of an eye, it was up and at him again. A mongrel with the muscles of a bear, it snarled and sprang.

Fargo was vaguely aware that Abner was running toward the farmhouse. Then he had to concentrate on the dog and only the dog. Its teeth sheared at his neck. Again he knocked it down but it streaked right back up. The animal was fast. He backpedaled, thinking to gain the second he needed to take aim.

The dog came after him. It bit at his leg and he dodged. It snapped at his wrist and he jerked his arm out of reach.

Abner was shouting something but Fargo couldn't make out what it was.

The mongrel crouched and snarled and vaulted high, again going for his throat.

Fargo swung the stock. It caught the dog on the head but hardly fazed it, and it chomped at his leg. Fargo kicked it.

The dog rolled and was up, its teeth bared.

This was taking too long. Any moment, Fargo realized, Abner would come out of the house with a gun. Fargo feinted going right. The dog lunged and he brought the stock down on the crown of its head. Not once but three times. The dog sprawled flat and didn't move.

A revolver cracked and lead buzzed Fargo's ear. He whirled and crouched to present less of a target.

Abner was on the porch, Fargo's Colt clutched in both hands, taking deliberate aim.

Fargo dived and the six-shooter cracked again. He heard the *thwack* of the slug as it struck the ground next to him.

Shouting "Damn you! Damn you!" Abner curled the hammer to try again.

Fargo centered the sights and steadied the barrel and shot him in the chest.

Jolted onto his heels, Abner tottered back and struck the wall.

In the doorway a woman screamed.

Abner raised the Colt, struggling to hold it still as he oozed down, his legs unable to support him. The hammer clicked and he said, "I've got you now, you son of a bitch."

Fargo shot him in the head. Brains and blood splattered and Abner folded like an accordion and fell onto his side. Rising, Fargo went up the steps.

A woman inside the screen door had her hand to her throat. Behind her were three children. "How could you?" she wailed.

Fargo remembered seeing her at Harold's farm and again at Belinda Jackson's. "You know damn well why," he said, and pulled the Colt loose from Abner's fingers.

"Pa!" a little girl cried. "Oh, Pa!"

Fargo leaned the Henry against the wall and reloaded the Colt. He was aware of their eyes on him, and their weeping, and when he was done he twirled the Colt into his holster and said, "Do you want me to bury him for you?"

"No," the woman said between sobs. "I want you to leave."

Fargo snatched the Henry and was ten steps across the yard when she called out to him and he stopped.

"Don't think you can get away with this, mister! I'm tellin' our kin! They'll be after you, Orville and the rest! You won't last a week."

"You've got it backwards, lady," Fargo said.

Confused, she wiped her face with a sleeve and said, "Backwards how?"

"They don't have to come after me."

"Why not?"

"Because I'm going after them." Fargo smiled and touched his hat and bent his steps to the Ovaro. Shoving the Henry into the scabbard, he straddled the saddle and departed.

The McWhertle farms were widely scattered. Most were within ten miles or so of Ketchum Falls but a few were farther out. Clyde McWhertle's was one of the latter. It could be reached only by following a long, winding road to the northwest.

Judging by the position of the Big Dipper, it was pushing midnight when Fargo got there. He figured everyone would be in bed but a single window glowed at the back. On the lookout for dogs, he rode around to almost within earshot, and drew rein.

He left the Henry in the scabbard and went to the window, careful that his spurs didn't jingle.

Clyde McWhertle was at the kitchen table, a nearly empty bottle of whiskey and a glass in front of him. His arms were folded and his head was on them. He appeared to have drunk himself into a stupor.

Near a corner of the house stood a maple. Fargo searched under it and found part of a downed limb that still had leaves.

Holding it by the broken end, Fargo returned to the window. He stood to one side so McWhertle couldn't see him and lightly swished the leaves on the glass. He did it five times. He did it ten.

It was the fourteenth when Clyde's head rose and he looked around in confusion.

Fargo did it once more.

Smacking his lips and scratching himself, Clyde shifted in his chair and looked at the window. When he didn't see anything he reached for the bottle and poured. Draining the glass, he wiped his mouth with the back of his hand.

Fargo ran the leaves over the glass and let the branch drop.

Clyde looked around, his expression one of puzzlement. He slowly stood, swaying. When he turned he nearly fell over the chair. Pushing it, he shambled to the door and worked a bolt and opened it.

"Is that you, you damned cat?"

Fargo slipped behind the door.

"You're a damned nuisance," Clyde said thickly, slurring his words. He stepped outside. "Where the hell are you? I have half a mind to kick you into next week."

Fargo stepped into the open. "Meow," he said.

Clyde turned.

Fargo unleashed an uppercut that sent him toppling. Clyde bleated and tried to rise but Fargo knocked him flat.

"Remember me?"

Clyde was struggling to focus. Between the liquor and the blows he was befuddled as hell. "You!" he finally blurted. "Here?"

"Do you recollect that beating you and your kin gave me?" Fargo asked.

"Orville told us to!"

"Then you can tell Orville this for me," Fargo said, and laid into him. Clyde tried to block the first few blows with no success. Throwing his arms over his head, he mewed and grunted as Fargo slammed fists to his gut and ribs. Fargo's last blow was to the groin.

Crying out, Clyde clutched himself and doubled over. "No more, mister," he begged.

Fargo cocked his fist.

"God in heaven, no more. I can't take it. Honest I can't." Clyde sniffled.

Fargo looked at his fist and slowly lowered it. "Abner is in hell," he announced.

"How's that?"

"You need to pay attention."

"I'm tryin'. But I had a little too much to drink. I do that a lot."

Fargo rapped him on the head. "Shake it off. Or do I have to beat on you more?"

"No! Please!"

"Your cousin Abner is dead. I blew his brains out."

"God Almighty. Why?"

"He tried to stave my ribs in. You should remember. You were right there at his side."

Clyde forgot his pain in his shock. "You miserable bastard."

"Save the name calling for later."

"Are you fixin' to kill me, too?"

Fargo shook his head. "I want you to go to Orville and tell him what I've done."

"You can count on that," Clyde said in fury. "I sure as hell won't waste a minute."

"Tell him it will get ugly from here on out."

"We'll give you ugly, mister," Clyde said. "We'll be after you, mister. Every last one of us. No one hurts a McWhertle and gets away with it. No one kills one of our clan and lives."

"You can see how scared I am."

"You will be," Clyde boasted. "Before we're done, you'll wish you had left when you could. But now it's too late. Killin' Abner was the same as slittin' your own throat."

Fargo half turned. "You can also let Orville know he won't have to bother looking for me."

"Why? Are you fixin' to tuck tail and run, after all?" Clyde scornfully asked.

"I'm fixing to pay Orville a visit."

"You're loco," Clyde said. "It's a wonder you're not foamin' at the mouth."

That reminded Fargo. "Where did Dogood and his van get to?"

"Charlie? He's stayin' the night out to Orville's, I think. Why?"

"He's on the list, too."

"What list are you talkin' about?"

"The list of sons of bitches who have this coming," Fargo said, and kicked him in the head.

# 22

Before daybreak Fargo was perched in a fork in a maple tree not thirty feet from Orville McWhertle's farmhouse. The Ovaro was back in the woods where no one was likely to come across it.

Clyde arrived half an hour before dawn. He'd ridden bareback and his horse was lathered. Sliding off, he stiffly went up the porch steps and pounded on the front door, hollering, "Orville! Orville! It's me! Open up, for God's sake."

The glow of a lamp lit an upstairs window. The curtains were apart, and Fargo saw Orville and Mabel hurry from the bedroom in their nightshirts, Mabel pulling a robe about her.

"Orville! Come on! It's important, damn it."

Even out in the maple Fargo heard the thump of Orville's heavy feet and then the front door was yanked wide.

"What in hell do you think you're doin'?" Orville roared, and grabbed his cousin by the throat. "Wakin' up my family this early—" He stopped.

Clyde was struggling to pry his cousin's thick fingers apart.

"What's happened to you? Your face is all swollen." Orville let go.

Clyde sucked in air and rubbed his neck. "Damn it, Orville. You had no cause to do that."

Orville stared at the lathered horse. "I reckon I lost my temper."

"Answer him," Mabel said to Clyde. "You look like you were stomped by a bull. What happened?"

"It was him," Clyde said, still rubbing his throat. "That Fargo feller."

"Hell," Orville said.

"He hurt me," Clyde bleated, "and sent me with a message. I can't hardly believe it's true but why would he have said it if'n it wasn't?"

"What message?"

"He told me Abner is dead."

Orville and Mabel looked at one another and both said at the same instant, "What?"

"That's right," Clyde confirmed, bobbing his head. "The son of a bitch claimed he killed him."

"You didn't think to swing by Abner's and make sure before you came here?" Orville angrily demanded.

"Hell, you know how far he lives from me," Clyde said sulkily. "Be glad I even made it here. I keep havin' these dizzy spells."

"Can it be true?" Mabel asked her husband.

Orville nodded. "I was afraid of this. Afraid this one was different."

"Different how?"

"Some men bend but never break," Orville said. "This scout has some thick bark."

"Forget him," Mabel said. "We need to find out about cousin Abner."

Just then the morning quiet was broken by the clatter of a buckboard. Raising a cloud of dust, it raced out of the gray gloom. Abner's wife was handling the team. The three kids were huddled fearfully in the bed.

"Why, that's Phyllis," Mabel said.

The buckboard slewed to a stop and Phyllis sprang down, barking at her brood, "Stay put, you hear?" She bounded up the steps. "You won't believe it!" she exclaimed.

"Your husband is dead," Orville said.

"How did you—?" Phyllis looked at Clyde. "Oh God. That devil paid you a visit, too?"

"Abner, dead?" Mabel said in disbelief. "Who does that son of a bitch think he is?"

"There's more," Phyllis said. "He told me to say that he's comin' for you, Orville."

"He told me to say the same thing," Clyde said.

"The nerve," Mabel declared. "We can't let this stand, Orville. We have to find him before he finds you. Call a gatherin' of the clan."

"Hush, woman. I'm thinkin'." Orville moved to the rail and gazed at his barn and then at the woods.

"What are you waitin' for?" Mabel impatiently demanded. "We need to act."

Orville turned. "Rouse Sam and Tyrell. Have them dress and come on down. I have errands for them."

Mabel nodded and hastened in.

"I feel awful," Clyde said. He leaned against the house and put his hands on his knees. "I'm woozy again. Damn him, anyhow."

"His days are numbered, cousin," Orville promised. "I was easy on him before but I won't be easy now."

"You'd think he'd have the sense to leave while he could," Phyllis said. Her eyes watered and she said, "I can't hardly believe my Abner is gone." She wrapped her arms around her bosom and broke into tears.

"Enough of that," Orville said. "Cry inside if you have to, and take your kids along." He held out a hand. "Wait. First tell me how he did it."

"He shot him. Twice. First in the chest and then in the head."

"What was Abner doin'?"

"Tryin' to shoot him, of course. Abner sicced our dog on him but the son of a bitch killed it, too. Stove its head in with his rifle butt."

"Grit to spare," Orville said.

"Quit soundin' as if you admire him," Phyllis snapped. "He's not one of us. He's not a McWhertle so he doesn't count. Your very words."

"He counts when it comes to killin' us," Orville said. "It's not that I admire him so much as I respect how easy he pulls the trigger. Most men can't or won't."

"Oh, he does that easy enough," Phyllis said bitterly. "I think he liked blowin' my Abner's brains out. I truly do." Gathering up her children, she went inside.

Clyde had a hand to his temple where Fargo had kicked him.

"I thought him and that doc would have the sense to leave and never come back."

"The doc will. Him we'll have to do the hard way," Orville said.

"I told him he's loco," Clyde said. "Told him he can't lick our whole clan."

"What did he say to that?"

"He asked me where Dogood got to." Clyde looked toward the barn. "Say, where did he get to, anyhow? I don't see his wagon anywhere."

"Charlie had a call he said he had to make," Orville said. "He left last night for town."

The door opened and out came two boys, one about sixteen, the other a few years younger. The oldest was pulling on a shirt, the youngest was barefoot.

"Ma said you wanted us."

Orville placed a hand on the shoulder of each. "Fetch your horses. You're to spread the word that the clan is to gather here by noon. No exceptions. Make sure they understand that. Anyone doesn't show, they'll answer to me."

Both boys quick-footed to the barn. They were inside only a couple of minutes before they reappeared on horseback and galloped past the house, waving to their pa as they went by.

Up in the tree Fargo leaned back and flexed one leg and then the other. He would be there a while. Movement in the bedroom window drew his attention. Mabel had shed her robe and nightdress and was getting dressed. She had tits the size of watermelons.

"Let's get you inside so you can rest," Orville said to Clyde. "You look plumb tuckered out."

"I do feel poorly," Clyde said.

Fargo settled into the fork. He was well screened by branches. Unless someone walked under the tree, it was unlikely he'd be seen. He figured it would be an hour or more before the first of the clan showed up but barely twenty minutes went by and three men trotted up. He recognized all three from town; they'd taken part in the tying and the tarring.

Singly and in groups, on horseback and in wagons, over the course of the morning the rest of the clan gathered. The house became filled to overflowing, the drone of voices was constant. Shortly before noon they filed out and assembled on the front lawn.

Orville didn't keep them waiting. Attended by his wife and Clyde, he stepped to the edge of the porch and raised his arms for quiet.

"By now all of you have heard. Abner is dead. We thought that tarrin' the doc and her friend would send them packin' but we were wrong."

"Let's find the bastard and do him in," a man hollered.

"That's why I sent for you," Orville said. "We'll split up into groups and hunt until we find him or we hear he's skedaddled, which I doubt."

"What do we do when we have him?"

"Need you ask? He's killed Abner. It's an eye for an eye, a life for a life."

"It's a good thing the marshal is dead so he can't try to stop us," someone said.

Orville didn't waste any more time. He divided the men into groups and gave each group a section of Coogan County to cover. He divided the women, as well, and sent them out in wagons and buckboards, along with their kids, to scour the roads and byways.

"If you spot him get word to the rest of us," Orville instructed them.

"How?" an older woman asked.

"Mabel and me will stay here with our boys," Orville said. "Come straightaway and we'll send Sam and Tyrell out to round up everyone else."

With a lot of enthusiastic whoops and yips, the McWhertle clan departed. Within five minutes the only ones left were Orville and his family. Orville stood watching the last of the wagons wind out of sight, then turned and ushered his wife and sons indoors.

Fargo waited another five minutes before he descended. He hadn't seen a dog anywhere so he felt safe in moving along the side of the house to the rear and peering in a window. It was the kitchen, and Mabel was at the counter, chopping carrots.

He could see the back door; it wasn't bolted.

Drawing his Colt, he gripped the latch and barreled in. Mabel turned and froze with a carrot in one hand and the knife in the other.

Fargo pointed the Colt at her face. "Put the knife down," he said quietly.

She didn't want to. Her posture warned him she was thinking of trying to stick him.

"You can put it down or I can put you down," Fargo said. He wouldn't shoot her. But after what she had done to Belinda, he wouldn't hesitate to rap her over the head with the barrel.

"Bastard," she said.

Fargo thumbed back the hammer. "Do it quiet. If your boys come running in here, who knows what will happen."

That got to her. Mabel set the knife down and smiled. "Happy now?"

"The carrot too." Fargo wouldn't it past her to try and poke his eye out.

She set it next to the knife.

"Where's Orville and your sons?"

"Last I saw they were in the parlor."

"Walk in front of me," Fargo directed. "Try to warn them and lead will fly."

"We should have killed you when we had the chance."

"Yes," Fargo said. "You should have." He touched the muzzle to the back of her head to forestall her acting up.

She behaved until they were almost there and then she suddenly ran ahead and shrieked at the top of her lungs, "Orville! He's here! Kill him!"

# 23

Fargo was expecting her to try something. He was right behind her as she burst into the parlor and took a bound to the left so he had a clear shot at everyone in it.

Orville McWhertle was in a chair by a fireplace. His two sons, Sam and Tyrell, were on the settee. All three rose as Mabel burst in and froze when they saw Fargo train the Colt.

Mabel stopped and glared at her husband and gestured at Fargo. "What are you waitin' for?"

Orville had eyes only for the Colt. "Be sensible, woman. He's armed and I'm not."

Fargo noticed both boys glance at the mantle; a rifle was propped against it. "You try and you'll die," he said. He also spied a box of lucifers.

"No one is goin' to try anythin'," Orville said pointedly.

"What is it you want, mister?"

"A keg of black powder," Fargo said, "but I'll settle for the four of you walking ahead of me out to the barn."

"What do we want to go there for?" Mabel demanded.

"Because I said so."

"Pa?" Tyrell said. He was fidgeting and the one who would make a play if he could.

"Do as he tells us for now, boy," Orville directed. "He won't shoot us so long as we do as he wants."

"He shot Abner," Mabel said.

"Didn't you hear Abner's wife?" Orville returned. "Abner was tryin' to kill him."

"I hate how you make him out to be worth a damn," Mabel said. "He's killed one of our own and deserves to have his wick snuffed out. Nothin' else matters."

"Breathin' does," Orville said. "We can't avenge Abner if we're dead."

Fargo cut their bickering short with, "Out to the barn. Orville, you go first. Then your wife. Then the boys."

"Why us last?" Sam demanded.

"So he can see you," Orville said. "If you were in front of me, I'd block his view."

"I hate this," Mabel said as she fell into step behind him. "I hate an outsider bossin' us around. And I hate your lack of gumption."

"Watch your mouth," Orville warned.

Fargo grabbed the lucifers from the mantle as he went out and shoved them in a pocket. As they crossed the yard he scanned the road. No one was in sight.

Ten milk cows were in the barn. So were a few chickens, pecking around.

"This is far enough," Fargo said. He told the boys to shoo all the cows and the chickens out.

"What on earth for?" Mabel asked. "We'll just have to round them up again later."

Ignoring her, Fargo said to the boys, "Hurry it up. I don't have all day."

They looked at their father and Orville nodded and they moved to the cows.

Orville stared at Fargo. "If you're up to what I think you are, it's petty."

"I could do a lot worse," Fargo said.

"It's for the tarrin', ain't it? The tarrin' and the beatin'?"

"I don't forgive and I don't forget."

"In the long run what does it get you? You can't fight all of us."

"So everyone keeps telling me." Fargo was watching the boys. They were behaving. One by one they hustled the cows out and when the last was gone he had them do the same with the chickens. Then he made them stand by their parents and stepped to a lantern hanging on a peg.

"What are you fixin' to do?" Mabel broke her silence. "It better not be what I think it is."

"In your next life," Fargo said, "get in the line for brains." He took down the lantern and moved to a pile of straw.

"Don't you dare," Mabel said.

Fargo dashed the lantern against the wall and sent a shower of broken glass and kerosene raining down on the straw.

"What's he doin', Pa?" Tyrell asked.

Orville was glowering, his big fists clenched. "What do you think he's doin'?" he growled.

"Oh God," Mabel said.

Fargo took the lucifers from his pocket. Squatting, he opened the box and plucked one of the sticks.

"Why, he's fixin' to set our barn on fire!" young Sam blurted.

"We have to stop him, Pa," Tyrell said.

"Barns can be rebuilt," Orville said.

Fargo struck the lucifer. Flame spurted, and he nearly sneezed at the odor. Tossing it into the straw, he kicked the box in after it and stepped well back. Right away the kerosene caught. Flames crackled and rapidly grew. Soon they were licking at the wall.

"Not our barn!" Mabel wailed, and turned to her husband. "Do somethin', you damn lump!"

Orville backhanded her. He knocked her flat and she lay in a daze with her mouth bleeding. "Don't ever talk to me like that again, woman. I won't have it, you hear?"

"But, Pa," Sam said.

"I won't take it from you, neither," Orville said, and nodded at Fargo. "Why do you think he's doin' this? To provoke us. To give him an excuse to shoot us. We go at him with our bare hands he'll shoot us in the arm or the leg. We go at him with a weapon and we're dead."

"You're not as dumb as she thinks you are," Fargo said.

"There's more to come, ain't there?" Orville said. "You aim to make all of us pay. Not just me but the whole clan."

"Like you said," Fargo replied, "an eye for an eye."

The flames climbed the wall toward the hayloft. Smoke was spreading in thick coils that writhed toward the rafters.

"Pick her up and move outside," Fargo commanded.

Orville bent and scooped his wife into his big arms. His sons moved to help but he motioned them away.

Within a few minutes one side of the barn was a sheet of flame and gray clouds rose from the roof.

Mabel angrily pushed away from Orville and said, "I'll never forgive you for this. Hittin' me and all."

"You don't behave, I'll hit you again," Orville said. "A female has to know her place."

"He's right, Ma," Sam said.

"What do you know? You're just a boy."

"Woman," Orville said ominously, "you are testin' my patience."

"And you test mine every day, treatin' me like I'm less than you."

"You are," Orville said. "You're female."

Mabel recoiled as if he had slapped her. "Is that the real reason you hate that lady doc so much? I thought it was to help out Charlie Dogood."

"It was both," Orville said. "I told you before. Doctorin' ain't for women. It's man's work."

"Why, you . . ." Mabel said, and seemed unable to find the right words.

Orville wheeled on her. "Enough. When I took you for my wife you pledged to honor and obey. Remember that obey part and shut the hell up before I get good and mad and wallop you again."

"You've never talked to me like this before," Mabel said, sounding hurt.

"You've never given me cause."

The fire was devouring the roof, with the sheets of flame rising higher than ever.

Fargo backed toward the woods.

"Hey, where's he goin', Pa?" Sam yelled.

"You can run but we'll find you," Orville called after him. "We won't rest until we do."

"Good," Fargo said. Turning, he jogged off.

At a growl from Orville, Sam and Tyrell bolted for the house.

By the time they came back out with rifles, Fargo was in the trees. Once on the Ovaro, he rode due east for half a mile and then reined to the north. In a while he came to a flat-crowned hill. From the top he could see the smoke. So could most everyone in the county. Grinning, he thrust two fingers into a pocket and pulled out a folded sheet of paper. On the crude map Belinda had drawn for him were eleven X's, each a McWhertle farm. It was as many as she could remember.

The next was two miles to the northeast as the crow flew. It belonged to one of those who beat him at Belinda's. Clarence was the man's name, and Fargo vividly recollected how Clarence had grinned while kicking him.

The farm was deserted. Clarence and his family were taking part in the search.

Fargo shooed half a dozen cows from the barn and set it on fire. Now two thick columns blackened the Arkansas air.

Fargo grinned to himself as he rode away. This was akin to poking a hornet's nest with a stick to rile the hornets, and he wanted the McWhertles good and riled. He wanted them so mad that they'd come gunning for him.

Some people, Fargo reflected, might say he was going to a lot of bother. If he wanted them dead, why not kill them outright? Why burn their barns and toy with them like a cat toying with mice?

Fargo had two reasons. First, he didn't go around killing in cold blood. But if he had to defend himself, that was different. The second reason was more personal; he *liked* toying with the sons of bitches. And the bitches. After what they'd done to Belinda and him, they had it coming.

In less than an hour two more columns were rising aloft.

The next farm was due west.

Fargo wasn't in any hurry. The Ozarks in the summer were gorgeous. The day was pleasant, the sun warm, the birds singing and butterflies flitting about.

He came to a creek and followed it to a grassy bank. There he drew rein. His body was so sore from the beating he took that climbing down hurt like hell. He let the Ovaro drink while he walked back and forth to stretch his legs.

The woods around him had gone quiet. He didn't think much of it until the stallion raised its head and stared intently into the forest.

Fargo turned. It could be anything. Deer, a bear, a bobcat. He wasn't concerned. Then, from the vicinity of a thicket, there came a hiss.

Fargo's skin prickled. Whipping out the Colt, he sidled toward the Ovaro. He'd become so caught up in his vendetta against the McWhertles that he'd forgotten about the rabies scare.

The vegetation shook and crackled and a figure lurched into the sunlight.

It was Old Man Sawyer. He was gaunt and pale, his clothes in tatters. Foam rimmed his mouth and his red eyes were swollen to twice their normal size. He sniffed the air like a wild beast, his face and neck muscles twitching.

Fargo stood stock still. The Ovaro wasn't moving, either, and the old man hadn't spotted them yet.

Sawyer shambled along in stiff, jerky movements. His arms were like boards and he seemed to move them with difficulty. He passed under the overspreading boughs of an oak and in another minute he would be out of sight.

The Ovaro nickered.

Instantly, Old Man Sawyer spun. His red eyes swung right and left and focused on the stallion—and on Fargo.

"Hell," Fargo said.

# 24

Old Man Sawyer screeched and rushed at Fargo with his arms spread. He uttered guttural grunts and growls and his fingers opened and closed.

Fargo skipped aside. Pivoting, he slammed the barrel against the old man's head and Sawyer buckled to his knees.

The old man hissed and twisted and clawed at Fargo's leg.

Eluding his grasp, Fargo hit him again. For most that would have been enough but the lunatic heaved to his feet and attacked.

Fargo ducked under hooked fingers and backpedaled. Sawyer kept coming and he thumbed back the hammer, about to shoot the old man in the head.

Unexpectedly, he got help from an unforeseen source: the Ovaro. Sawyer had fallen near the stallion. Now, as he ran past it, the Ovaro lashed out with its rear hooves. One caught the madman in the back and sent him crashing into a tree.

Sawyer hit it with a loud crack, managed a couple of tottering steps, and collapsed.

For a few moments Fargo thought the old man was dead.

Then Sawyer got his hands under him and sought to rise. He couldn't. Sinking flat, Sawyer closed his eyes, his chest rising and falling with apparent effort.

Fargo stood over him. It would be an act of kindness, he reckoned, to put the old man out of his misery. He aimed between Sawyer's eyes. "It has to be done," he said out loud.

He was curling his finger around the trigger when the last thing he imagined would happen, happened—Sawyer talked.

"Who are you?" he said weakly.

"Sawyer?"

The man opened his eyes. His mindless fury had faded and in

its place was shock and confusion. "Who are you?" he gasped again. "Where am I?"

"You don't know?"

Sawyer had to try several times before he said, "If I knew, would I ask?"

Fargo lowered the Colt. The whitish froth was no longer oozing from the old man's mouth. "You've been running around the countryside for a couple of days trying to bite people."

"Are you loco?" Sawyer said. "I'd never do a thing like that."

Fargo warily hunkered at arm's length. "You would if you were foaming at the mouth."

"What are you tryin' to say? That I have rabies and I didn't know it?"

"You have something," Fargo said. He'd never heard of a rabies victim as far gone as Sawyer had been recovering enough to hold a conversation.

"I don't savvy," Sawyer said. He bent his head and looked down at himself. "Good God. There's blood all over me. How can this be?"

"I just told you."

"I don't have rabies," Sawyer said. "If I did, don't you think I'd know it?"

"Not if it came on you sudden," Fargo said. "Think back. Were you bit by a wild animal a while ago?"

"Hell no," Sawyer said. "I'd never let a wild critter get close enough."

"When you were sleeping, maybe?" Fargo said. "A coon that snuck into your cabin."

"No, I tell you I might be old but I ain't stupid. An animal hasn't bit me in so long, I can't remember when."

"You killed all of yours."

Sawyer tried to sit up and sank down with groan. "What was that again?"

"Your dog. Your mule. Your chickens," Fargo said. "You killed every last one. I saw them with my own eyes when I took Dr. Jackson out to your cabin."

"Doc Jackson?" Sawyer said. "I'm not one of her patients. Why would she come way out to my place?"

"I reckon she thought it was the right thing to do," Fargo answered.

Sawyer closed his eyes. His body quaked and his limbs shook

in a fit that lasted several minutes. When it was over, he lay limp and caked with sweat. "I reckon you're right. I am sick."

"I can take you to the doc's if you think you can hold out," Fargo said. He didn't mention that he'd have to bind and gag him.

"Would it do me any good?"

Fargo was honest with him. "I don't know."

Sawyer gazed in confusion at the sky. "If only I could make sense of this."

"Do you remember biting Abigail McWhertle?"

"The hell you say."

"She ran around foaming at the mouth too until her cousins drowned her."

"They *murdered* her?"

"Her and her folks. Timmy Wilson came down with it and he's dead too."

"I knew young Tim. He was in town when I . . ." Sawyer shuddered anew and closed his eyes. His breathing grew shallow, his chest hardly moved.

Fargo sensed the old man was close to death's door. "If you could remember what bit you."

"Nothin' did, damn it. How many times do I have to say the same thing?" Sawyer gnawed his lower lip. "Let me think on this some."

"Don't take too long," Fargo advised. He took a chance and gripped the old man's wrist. The arm was skin and bone. He found a pulse; it was weak and fluttering.

Several minutes went by and Sawyer didn't move or speak.

Just when Fargo thought the old man would never speak again, Sawyer fooled him and opened his eyes.

"Listen, mister. I've done thought about it and thought about it and I think I have the answer."

"Tell me."

"Bend down. It takes too much out of me to try and talk loud."

Fargo would rather stick his head in a grizzly's maw but he bent until his ear was inches from the old man's mouth. He tried not to think of the consequences should Sawyer begin foaming again and take a bite out of him. The stink of the man's breath was abominable. He held his own and said, "I'm listening."

In a ragged whisper, his voice fading at times, Sawyer imparted his information.

"Son of a bitch," Fargo said when the old man finished. "I had my suspicions." He placed his hand on Sawyer's shoulder. "Dr. Jackson needs to know. I'll hoist you up on my saddle and we'll light a shuck."

Sawyer's eyes were intent on the sky.

"Did you hear me?" Fargo said. When he got no answer, he felt for a pulse again. There wasn't any. He closed the old man's eyelids and said, "Damn."

Fargo took the time to scoop a shallow grave. He piled rocks and tree limbs on the mound of dirt to discourage scavengers, and forked leather. He was through burning barns. He had something more important to do.

It was evening when the lights of Ketchum Falls sparkled like so many fireflies. With the McWhertles out to get him, he didn't dare show himself on the main street. He stuck to the back ways.

Belinda's house was quiet. A few lights were on and her shadow moved across a second floor window.

The gate in the picket fence squeaked when Fargo opened it. He led the Ovaro in and closed the gate and went to the back steps. He knocked and waited but she didn't come so he knocked louder. When she still didn't appear, he tried the latch. The door wasn't locked. Entering, he called out, "Belinda?" He didn't get an answer.

Fargo closed the door and crossed the kitchen and went along the hall to the foot of the stairs. "Belinda?" he hollered again.

"Up here." Her voice was muffled.

Fargo went up them three at a stride and stopped at the landing. "Are you in your bedroom?"

The door across from her bedroom opened and out stepped Clyde McWhertle with a rifle in his hands. "No," he smirked. "She's not."

After him came two others with rifles.

"Where's Belinda?" Fargo demanded.

"Belinda, is it?" Clyde said, and tapped on her bedroom door. "Come on out and show him."

A middle-aged woman emerged. She smirked as broadly as Clyde.

"This is my cousin, Felicia. She's the one answered you and made you think she was the doc."

"Did I do good, cousin?" she asked.

"You did good," Clyde praised her.

Fargo repeated his question. "Where's Belinda Jackson?"

"The doc is bein' took care of," Clyde said. "As for you, Orville reckoned you'd show here sooner or later so he sent me and these others. We've been waitin' most of the day."

Footsteps below alerted Fargo to others of the clan who had been hiding in the parlor and elsewhere.

"Pretty clever, our cousin Orville," Felicia crowed.

"He's powerful mad at you, mister," a man behind Clyde said. "You burnin' down his barn and all."

"And mine, I hear," Clyde said venomously. "My missus and young'uns are out there now. She was worried you'd burn down our house, too."

"His burnin' days are over," Felicia declared.

"All his days are over," the same man said.

Fargo wanted to kick himself for walking right into their trap. "What did you mean by Belinda being taken care of?"

"Wouldn't you like to know?" Felicia mocked him, and laughed.

"Exactly what I said," Clyde replied. "She's bein' took care of by Charlie Dogood."

Without thinking Fargo started to turn, only to have several muzzles trained on his chest.

"I wouldn't be hasty," Clyde said.

"We shouldn't be talkin' like this," one of the men remarked. "Orville warned you how sneaky he is. We're supposed to hog-tie him and take him to Orville's."

"Fetch a rope," Clyde said.

A McWhertle down the stairs nodded and made for the front door.

Felicia regarded Fargo like a cat might a canary. "It beats me why you didn't fan the breeze when you had the chance. Are you and the doc foolin' around together? Is that why you're so anxious to help her? The little hen."

"I'd rather fool around with her any day than a cow like you," Fargo said to get her goat, and it worked.

Felicia colored. Raising her hand to slap him, she stepped in front of Clyde.

"Felicia, don't," Clyde warned.

Fargo punched her. He drove his fist into her gut and shoved her against Clyde and the other two and all three lost their balance and stumbled.

Down the stairs a woman yelled too late, "Look out!"

Springing past Felicia before anyone could shoot, Fargo darted into Belinda's bedroom and slammed the door. Dashing to a chair, he wedged it against the door. "Anyone tries to come in," he shouted, drawing his Colt, "will take lead."

To his surprise, Clyde McWhertle laughed. "Mister, you're stupid as can be. Have you looked out the window?"

Fargo edged over and risked a peek. More of them were out in front, another seven or eight.

"You see our kinfolk out there?" Clyde yelled.

"I see them."

Clyde laughed merrily. "How does it feel to be trapped?"

# 25

Skye Fargo did a strange thing, a thing that if Clyde McWhertle had seen, he wouldn't understand. Fargo smiled.

Then he went to the door but stayed to one side in case they fired through it. "Where did Dogood take Dr. Jackson?"

On the other side Clyde snickered. "We've got you surrounded and that's what you want to know?"

"Where?"

"We aim to be shed of her, permanent, so Charlie took her where no one would suspect."

"Where?" Fargo asked again.

"That's for us to know and you to figure out," Clyde taunted. "Now then. Why don't you be smart and surrender? Throw out your smoke wagon and we promise not to shoot."

"Why would I do that?" Fargo said, "when I have you where I want you?"

"*You* have *us*?" Clyde said, and cackled. "Mister, if I had any doubts before, I don't now. You're plumb loco."

"Let me hear you drop your rifles and there won't be any blood spilled," Fargo said. As he did, he quietly moved the chair he had propped against the door.

"We outnumber you fifteen to one and you're askin' us to surrender?" Clyde laughed. "You know what I might do? Just for the fun of it? Since you saw fit to burn down my barn and a bunch of others, I'm thinkin' it would be, what do they call it, poetical justice if I burned down the doc's house with you inside. How would that be?"

"There's a flaw in your brainstorm," Fargo said.

"I'm all ears," Clyde replied.

"No," Fargo said, "you're all stupid." He threw open the door and caught them flat-footed with their rifle barrels pointed at the floor.

Clyde swore and tried to bring his rifle up and Fargo shot him in the face. He drove his shoulder into Felicia, slamming her against the wall. He punched a man in the jaw and kicked another in the knee. Then he was at the landing and looked back as another McWhertle whipped a rifle to his shoulder. He shot the man in the chest.

At the bottom of the stairs were three more. Two had rifles. He was halfway down when he had to put lead into one and he was almost to the bottom when he had to shoot the other.

A woman shrieked and tried to grab him and he gave her the same he would give a man: a solid right to the chin.

The hall to the kitchen was clear but the kitchen wasn't and as he burst into it, two men were rising from the table. He moved so fast he was on them before they could lift their rifles. He smashed the Colt against the ear of one and punched the other in the throat.

The back door wasn't bolted. As he flew into the night shouts and curses broke out. He reached the Ovaro and swung on.

Reining toward the front, he galloped the length of the house. Only a few McWhertles were in the front yard. The rest had run inside when they heard the shooting. A beefy man elevated a shotgun and Fargo shot him. Another raised a rifle and Fargo shot him. A woman pulled a pocket pistol from a purse and he shot her.

Then the Ovaro was in the street and Fargo reined toward the center of town. He figured they would be less likely to shoot at him with townsfolk around but he was wrong.

Fireflies flared in the dark and the boom of thunder was near constant. Lead whistled and sizzled. Fortunately the dark caused them to misjudge their aim, or else they were just piss-poor shots.

At a junction Fargo reined right. At the next he reined left. There were fewer lights and few people and no one fired at him. He headed out of Ketchum Falls on the road that would eventually end at Old Man Sawyer's. At that hour there were few travelers and he had the road to himself. He looked back a few times but didn't see pursuit.

Fargo slowed to spare the stallion. He had made it out alive but the McWhertles would want to change that. They wouldn't be content with tarring and feathering. They'd be out for blood. Which suited him just fine. He had held back for too long. It came of not being a coldhearted killer. He needed to be provoked; he needed to have his life in peril.

Where many would be beside themselves having to shoot or be

142

shot at, Fargo was used to it. He was used to life on the frontier, where survival went to the quick and the strong. He was used to enemies like the Apaches, who never asked for mercy, or gave it. He was used to Sioux and Blackfeet on the warpath and out to lift his scalp unless he sent them into their hereafter.

Fargo remembered to reload. He didn't rightly know why he had gone this way, other than a vague feeling that he should.

It was only when the orchard hove out of the night that he had a sense of where his intuition had brought him. He reined up the lane and went through the apple trees and stopped when he set eyes on the farmhouse. Lights were on.

The patent medicine man's van was parked in front.

Fargo stopped and alighted. He left the stallion in shadow and cat-footed to the van. The team was dozing. One pricked its ears but neither whinnied. He went up the steps to the porch.

The front door was half open.

Fargo slipped inside. With his back to a wall, he crept to the parlor. It was empty. He continued to the kitchen. It was empty.

Up on the second floor someone said something.

Fargo was halfway up the stairs when he heard the voice again. It came from Harold and Edna's bedroom. He dropped into a crouch. It wouldn't do to be careless. More than his life was at stake.

". . . not how I wanted this to end," Charlie T. Dogood was saying. "I was content to have you leave Coogan County. But no. You had to be stubborn. You had to exhibit your silly female pride."

"I have as much right to be here as you do," Belinda Jackson said.

"There you go again. You never listen, my dear. For how long now have the McWhertles been saying that they don't want you in Ketchum Falls?"

"At your instigation," Belinda said.

Dogood chuckled. "I'll admit to a certain degree of manipulation, yes. But you can't hardly blame me, can you, given that until you arrived, I was the preeminent medical authority in this county, if not in all of the Ozarks."

Fargo stopped at the doorway.

Belinda was bound wrists and ankles and lay on her side on the floor. Dogood was perched on the edge of the bed. Two prone forms covered by sheets were behind him.

Harold and Edna, Fargo reckoned. He was about to barge in when Belinda spoke.

"A lot of people still look up to you as their healer. A lot still come to you for remedies."

"A lot but not all," Dogood said. "The first year you were here, my income dropped by a third."

"I'm sorry."

"Spare me your false sympathy. You took a lot of my business away from me, woman, and I resent it. I resent it no end."

"You could have moved on," Belinda said.

"Oh, you smug bitch," Dogood said. "I was here first. I practiced my trade in these mountains for damn near fifteen years before you showed up. But *I'm* supposed to move on and you get to stay."

"Charlie, we both know your so-called medicines are anything but. You concoct them out of whatever is handy."

"You have no proof of that."

"Ah, but I do," Belinda said, and smiled. "I sent a couple of your remedies to a chemist. One was a bottle of your cure for female complaints. Would you like to see his report? Your so-called medicine was eighty percent grain alcohol and ten percent opium mixed with ginger and mineral oil."

"Not bad," Dogood said. "He got almost all of them."

"Almost?"

"He missed the senna and turpentine."

Belinda raised her head. "Senna is a laxative. I can understand using that. But turpentine? What medicinal use does that have?"

"None," Dogood admitted, "other than to give it a little extra kick going down."

"Oh, Dogood," Belinda said.

"Don't get on your medical high horse with me," Charlie snapped. "A lot of my cures work and you damn well know it."

"What they do is dull the patient's suffering while the patient's own body heals itself," Belinda accused him. "You're no miracle worker."

"Neither are you, my dear." Dogood sighed and stood. "And now look at what your stubbornness has brought us to."

"Mine? What about your own?"

"I tried to be reasonable," Dogood said. "I've asked you politely a hundred times to ply your doctoring somewhere else. But you've refused. And now this rabies business has taught me that the only way to get rid of you is to, well, to get rid of you."

"You plan to kill me?"

"No, my dear. Your friend will."

"Friend?" Belinda said. "Do you mean Mr. Fargo?"

"I do indeed. You see, he's been running around setting McWhertle barns on fire. So no one will think twice if Harold's barn goes up in flames"—Dogood paused—"and the fire happens to spread to this house."

"You wouldn't," Belinda said.

"Can you think of a more perfect means? Everyone will think that Harold and Edna and Abby perished in the blaze. No one will suspect they were dead before the fire started."

"And me? How will you explain that?"

"The noble Dr. Jackson perished trying to save her patients." Dogood laughed.

"You're despicable."

"Now, now. Think of the adulation that will be heaped on you. Your sacrifice, your devotion, will be praised to high heaven. Your funeral should be well attended."

"One last question," Belinda said. "What about Fargo? What do you have planned for him?"

"I couldn't care less about him," Dogood answered. "But Orville, now, is fit to be tied. His kin are scouring the entire county for your buckskin-clad Romeo."

"And if they find him?"

"You might have noticed the violent streak that runs through the McWhertles. For the aggravation he's caused them, I'm afraid they intend to bed him with the worms."

Fargo stepped into the doorway. "They're trying their damnedest," he said.

Dogood started and took a step back. "You!" he blurted. "Here?"

"No. I'm back in town," Fargo said.

"How did you know where I was?"

"Luck," Fargo said, and motioned. "Suppose you untie her so we can get the hell out of here."

"Whatever you want. Just don't shoot." Dogood squatted and set to work on the knots. "This might take a while. Clyde tied her good and tight."

"Clyde is no longer with us," Fargo said. He would have related more but a hard object was jammed against the back of his head and a gun hammer clicked.

"Surprise, surprise," a woman said.

Dogood stopped prying and chuckled. "Thank you, my dear. Now we have both of them exactly where we want them."

# 26

Fargo looked over his shoulder. She looked to be all of twenty, if that, with long black hair and brown eyes.

Most would describe her as "plain." She wore a simple cotton dress of a style popular with farmers. Her eyes were twinkling and the hand that held a derringer pointed at his head was steady.

"Want me to shoot him, Charlie?"

"Not unless I say to or he gives us cause."

The young woman looked disappointed. She kept the derringer pointed and coughed and sniffled.

Dogood grinned and came over and held out his hand to Fargo. "Your Colt, if you please, and even if you don't, you buckskin-clad bumpkin."

Fargo was debating if he could spin and shoot her before she shot him. Something warned him not to try.

"She'll do it, you know," Dogood said. "Clementine will do anything I ask her."

Clementine giggled. "I surely will. Charlie only has to snap his fingers and I'll put a hole in your head."

"Killed before, have you?" Fargo stalled.

"Should I tell him, Charlie?" Clementine said.

"No," Charlie said, and waggled his fingers. "I won't ask you again, sir."

Reluctantly, Fargo gave him the Colt.

"Move over by the doc, there," Dogood said.

Not taking his eyes off Clementine, Fargo sidestepped to Belinda. "Guess I was careless."

"How were you to know about her?" Belinda said. "I only learned of their attachment on the way out here."

"Attachment?" Fargo said.

Dogood chortled and stood next to the young woman and put

his arm around her shoulders. "Clementine, here, is sweet on me, as they say in these parts."

"Powerful sweet," Clementine confirmed, and coughed a few times. "Have been for, what, eight or nine years now." She giggled. "My pa would have a fit if he knew. Which is why we keep it secret."

"Who is your pa?" Fargo asked. Not that he cared. So long as he kept them talking they might make a mistake.

"Orville McWhertle."

Suddenly Fargo gave a damn. He looked at the patent medicine man and then at Clementine. "You're old enough to be her father yourself."

"That I am," Dogood acknowledged with pride. "Yet she adores me anyway."

Clementine nodded. "It started when I went to see him for my female complaints. I was twelve and they'd just started and they hurt some." She grinned. "Well, one thing led to another, and . . ." She beamed at her sweetheart, and sniffled.

"God, no," Belinda said to Dogood. "You took advantage of a little girl?"

"She wasn't so little," Dogood said. "Fact is, she was big for her age."

"That's right," Clementine said. "I was practically a woman."

"It wasn't as if I was out to seduce her," Dogood said defensively. "It just sort of happened, and the next thing I knew, we were in love."

"Do I hear violin music?" Fargo said.

"Mock us if you must," Dogood said, giving Clementine a squeeze and kissing her on the cheek, "but ours is a love that will endure forever."

"A man your age," Belinda said. "You should be ashamed of yourself. You are the lowest of the low."

"That'll be enough out of you about him," Clementine said, and coughed. "It's your damn fault we're still here."

"I beg your pardon?" Belinda said.

"Him and me," Clementine said, dabbing at her nose with her sleeve. "He promised to take me to New Orleans. We'd buy us a house and live like man and wife. But first he needs to save up money and he can't save it as fast as we'd like with you takin' his patients away like you done."

"You do know he's stringing you along?" Belinda said. "He's just using that as an excuse."

Dogood squeezed Clementine's elbow. "Don't listen to her, my dear. She'll say anything to belittle me in your eyes."

"I can't wait for her to be out of the way," Clementine said.

Fargo was pondering something else. "You sure your pa doesn't know about the two of you?" he asked her.

Both of them looked uneasy and Clementine said, "What's that to you?"

"How about your mother?"

Clementine took a step and pointed her derringer at Fargo's head. "I've about had enough of you."

"Hold on, my dear," Dogood said. "We don't want bullet holes in either of them, remember? It must appear to be an accident of their own devising."

"I don't like him talkin' about my folks," Clementine said. "You know how they are."

To Fargo Dogood said, "Orville and Mabel would skin me alive if they knew. We've had to sneak around behind their backs all this time. Right now they think she is off with some of her cousins, searching for you."

"Interesting," Fargo said.

"You don't fool me," Dogood declared. "You're thinking that if you tell Orville about us, he'll turn on me and run me out of Coogan County, or worse."

Fargo sensed a note of fear. "Worse would be my guess," he said. "A lot worse."

"Let me shoot him," Clementine said. "I want her and him dead so much."

"Patience," Dogood replied. "Watch him while I fetch rope from my wagon. I'll be right back." He hastened out.

Fargo didn't like how Clementine's hand was twitching. "Easy on that trigger, girl."

"Call me a girl one more time," Clementine said. "I dare you."

Belinda cleared her throat. "If you don't mind my saying, you deserve better than Charlie Dogood."

"I do mind," Clementine said, sniffling. "The both of you hush up until he gets back."

"I'll hush if you'll answer a question that's not about you and him," Fargo said.

"Go ahead and ask then."

"How long have you been sick?"

"I ain't sick. I got me a cold, is all."

"How long have you had it?"

"I don't know. A week or so, I reckon. What the hell does it matter?"

"Has Dogood given you anything for it?"

"You said one question," Clementine said, and did more loud sniffling. "That makes three."

"Has he?"

"I've taken some stuff, yes," Clementine said. "Have been for a few days now."

"How do you feel after you take it?"

Clementine began tapping her foot in anger, and coughed. "I'm commencin' to not like you a whole lot. You're a blamed nuisance, is what you are."

"Do you break out in a sweat and your belly hurts for a while?"

"I do get a little sweaty, yes, but—" Clementine cocked her head. "Say now. What's this about?"

"Yes," Belinda said. "What are you getting at?"

"Timmy Wilson had a cold, remember?" Fargo said.

"Yes. I remember he was coughing and his nose was running that time he tried to rob us."

"Timmy did what, now?" Clementine said. She coughed some more.

"Why are their colds important?" Belinda asked.

"Old Man Sawyer had one too. He was so stuffed up he could hardly breathe."

"How do you know that?"

"He told me," Fargo said, and gave a short recital of his encounter. "He didn't have rabies. He wasn't bitten by anything that had it. It was the medicine he was taking." He looked at Clementine. "The medicine your lover gave him."

"You're tryin' to rile me."

"It fits," Fargo said. "Old Man Sawyer came down with something and Dogood sold him medicine. A few days after, Sawyer came down with fever and the shakes and started to foam at the mouth."

"You're lyin'."

"Timmy Wilson came down with a bad cold and Dogood sold

150

him the same medicine and a few days later Timmy ran amok in town."

"Stop it," Clementine said, and coughed.

"I bet Abigail was given the same medicine," Fargo said. "And now you."

"But I'm not foamin' at the mouth," Clementine said, and smirked. "So much for turnin' me against Charlie."

"You don't start foaming right away. Sawyer said it took four or five days."

"It won't work," Clementine told him.

"What could he be putting in his medicine?" Belinda wondered.

"You're the sawbones. You tell me."

Belinda wriggled onto her back, her worry transparent. "It could be any number of toxins. Either he doesn't care or he's unaware of the properties of his ingredients."

"Stop talkin' about Charlie like that," Clementine said, and sniffled. "He cares for folks. He'd never poison 'em. And he sure as blazes wouldn't poison *me*."

"He cares about the money he makes," Fargo said.

"That will be enough, goddamn it." Clementine sniffled and pointed the derringer at Belinda instead. "Go ahead and talk Charlie down again and see if I don't put lead between the doc's pretty eyeballs. Just you see if I don't."

Fargo stayed quiet. He wasn't about to tempt fate.

"That's better," Clementine said. "You're finally showin' some sense."

Ignoring her, Belinda said to Fargo, "If what you've said is true, there's no telling how many people he's infected."

"Stop it," Clementine said.

"I knew it wasn't rabies," Belinda said. "It didn't fit the symptoms."

"It wasn't Charlie," Clementine declared, and coughed almost violently. Her forehead was slick with sweat and her cheeks were specked with tiny red dots.

"You don't look well," Belinda said. "You don't look well at all."

"Shut the hell up."

"Trust me when I say I have your best interests at heart. I only want to help you."

"Damn you to hell. You people don't listen worth shucks." Clementine swore and kicked Belinda in the gut.

Fargo raised a hand to push Clementine away and found himself looking down the barrel of her derringer.

"Give me an excuse."

They stood like that until shoes thumped in the hall and Dogood returned carrying a coiled rope. He took one look and said, "What on earth is going on here, my dear?"

"Your sweetheart doesn't like to hear the truth," Fargo said.

"Has he been filling your head with lies about me?" Dogood asked her.

"Not you," Fargo said. "Your medicine."

"My nostrums do what I claim," Dogood said. "I have glowing testimonials from people I've cured to prove it. In writing, I might add. I have them in my van."

Clementine sniffled. "These two say you add stuff you shouldn't to your cures. Poisons, like, and you might not even know it." She swiped an arm at her nose. "Tell them, Charlie. Tell them you'd never do a thing like that."

"I'd never poison anyone," Dogood said.

"See?" Clementine said to Fargo and the doctor. "I told you. My man can tell you every ingredient he's ever added to any medicine he sells."

"Well, not every one," Dogood said.

"How's that again?"

"I like to experiment, my love. Sometimes I mix things in to see what they will do."

Clementine looked at him—and a small trickle of drool leaked from the corner of her mouth.

# 27

Dogood didn't notice. He was focused on Fargo and Belinda.

The rope was in his left hand; his right was on Fargo's Colt, which was wedged under his belt. "I'm always looking to improve my cures," he continued. "I'll add more alcohol. Or more opium. Or use cocaine instead. Or herbs I hear the Indians use. Or mushrooms I find out in the woods."

"Do you realize the risks you take?" Belinda asked in horror.

"Don't you start," Dogood said.

"All these years you've been playing with fire and now it has burned you," Belinda said.

Fargo was the only one watching Clementine. Drool now trickled from both corners of her mouth and her face was twitching. "The medicine that you sold Old Man Sawyer and Timmy and Abigail for their colds," he said. "What was in it?"

"A new and improved version of my cough elixir," Dogood boasted.

"What was new about it?"

"A colleague told me about a variety of water celery the Osage Indians use. I just happened to find some so I dried the root and ground it into a powder and added it. That, and some mushrooms I came across."

"Water celery?" Belinda said. "Are you sure you found the right kind? Some are part of the Apiaceae family."

"The what?"

"Hemlock," Belinda said. "My God. If you mixed that with certain types of mushrooms, there's no telling what would happen."

"You're trying to blame me for Sawyer and Tim and Abby," Dogood said. "But it won't wash. I've sold the same elixir to others and none of them took to running around the countryside biting folks."

"You sold some to Clementine, didn't you?" Fargo said.

"Sell a cure to my sweetheart?" Dogood grinned. "I should say not. I gave her a bottle free. In fact, she finished off the first and I gave her a second."

Belinda glanced at the girl, saying, "Clementine, have you noticed any unusual—" She stopped and gasped. "God in heaven."

"What are you on about?" Dogood said, and looked over his shoulder. He gasped, took a step back, and bleated, "Oh, please, no, no, no."

They had seen what Fargo already knew: Clementine McWhertle had undergone a transformation. White froth spilled from her lips, and her eyes, which were open again, were so bloodshot that the whites appeared red. Her face was still twitching and the muscles in her body were like taut wire. She seemed to have forgotten she was holding the derringer and her hand had dropped to her side.

"Clementine, dearest?" Dogood said. "Are you all right?"

Clementine hissed.

For a moment the tableau was frozen. Then Clementine crouched and let go of the derringer and hooked her fingers as if they were claws.

"Fight it, dear heart," Dogood said. "Get hold of yourself."

Baring her teeth, Clementine sprang at him.

So did Fargo. He grabbed for his Colt but Dogood shrieked and shoved him just as Clementine pounced. He screamed as she sheared her teeth into his neck.

"Skye, help me!" Belinda cried, struggling against her bonds.

Fargo didn't hesitate. She was helpless there on the floor. Bending, he slid his hands under her arms and dragged her toward the door.

Dogood was screeching and trying to prevent Clementine from biting him again. "Kill her!" he wailed, blood streaming from his wound. "Kill her! Kill her!"

Clementine had hold of his hair and his shirt and was snapping her teeth.

Fargo vaulted Belinda out and slammed the door behind them. He lifted her and made for the stairs but changed his mind. A bedroom was down the hall to the left. Entering, he shut the door, carefully laid Belinda on the bed, and reached into his boot for the Arkansas toothpick. "I'll have you free in a second."

"Did you see?" Belinda said, aghast. "That fool! That wretched, ignorant fool."

Fargo didn't need to ask which one she was referring to. He cut the rope binding her wrists and bent and did the same to the rope around her ankles.

From down the hall came a scream of terror.

"She's killing him," Belinda said, rubbing her wrists. "We have to help."

"He has it coming," Fargo said.

"Who are we to judge?" Belinda tried to push by to reach the door.

"We go out there, she'll attack us," Fargo said.

"What would you suggest? We hide in here and hope she leaves? If she gets away she'll attack others. I don't know about you but I don't want that on my conscience." Belinda shook her head. "No, I'm a physician. I have to help Dogood whether I want to or not."

"I'll go first," Fargo said.

The house had gone quiet. Quietly working the latch, he cracked the door enough to peer down the hall. It was empty. He couldn't tell if the other bedroom door was open or closed. Easing out, he crept toward it.

Belinda was beside him, her hand on his wrist. "Do you hear anything?" she whispered.

"Quiet, damn it." Fargo remembered how Timmy and Sawyer and Abigail had reacted to the slightest sounds.

The other door was shut. That meant Clementine was still in there.

Fargo put his ear to it. The silence baffled him. The afflicted were always hissing and couldn't stand still for two seconds.

"What are you waiting for?" Belinda whispered.

Fargo gave her a sharp look and she silently mouthed the words, "I'm sorry." Gingerly working the latch, he firmed his grip on the toothpick and pushed the door in.

Belinda put a hand to her mouth and said in dismay, "Oh, no."

Charlie T. Dogood's days of selling nostrums to the people of the Ozarks were over. He was slumped against the far wall, his throat ripped open, his shirt glistening scarlet. His eyes mirrored his shock. His mouth was open and his tongue stuck out; the tip had been bitten off.

Clementine wasn't anywhere to be seen.

"Where is she?" Belinda whispered.

Fargo was wondering the same thing. Squatting, he peered under the bed. She wasn't there. He straightened and checked behind the door. She wasn't there. Motioning to Belinda to stay put, he stalked to the closet and yanked it open.

She wasn't there, either. Perplexed, he turned and nearly collided with Belinda. "If you ever do as I want you to, the shock will kill me."

"How can you joke at a time like this?" Belinda said, staring sadly at Dogood.

"He got what he deserved."

"So you keep saying. But no one deserves *that*."

The curtain rustled, and Fargo whirled. But it was only the breeze. He realized the window was open but it had been shut before. Going over, he parted it with the toothpick and warily stuck his head out. Only a few feet below was the porch overhang. "She went out this way."

"She could be anywhere," Belinda said.

The barn was dark, the orchard a grotesque menagerie of silhouettes, the rest of the farm shrouded in ink.

"Wonderful," Fargo said.

"We have to go after her," Belinda said. "We have to find her and stop her before she hurts anyone else."

"There's only one way to stop her."

"Must we be so drastic? I was thinking we could take her alive."

"We?"

She nodded. "So I can subject her to tests and try to come up with a cure."

"Belinda . . ."

"I know. You're about to say I'm not being realistic. But as I keep having to remind you, I took an oath to heal people, not to kill them."

"You could end up like Charlie, there."

"It's a risk I'm willing to take."

Fargo stepped to Dogood and reclaimed his Colt. It was spattered with blood and he got some on his hand. He wiped the Colt on the patent medicine man's pants and his hand on his own and said, "I'm not."

"Two people have a better chance of subduing her than one."

"No."

"I can help. I can watch your back. And I promise to do exactly as you say."

Fargo looked at her.

"I can try."

"No."

Belinda wasn't happy. "You're terribly pigheaded. Has anyone ever told you that?"

"Every female who ever got to know me." Fargo closed the window and pulled the curtains and went around the bed. "Keep the door shut."

"Damn it, Skye. This is a woman's life we're talking about. Now that I know what Dogood mixed in his concoction, I might be able to help her."

"If I can take her alive, I will." Fargo started to back out.

"You promise? You give me your solemn word?"

"Aren't they the same?" Fargo almost had the door shut when she addressed him again.

"Be careful. As much as I want to save that girl, I don't want anything to happen to you."

"Even though I'm pigheaded?"

"You're male. You can't help it."

Fargo sighed and shut the door. He had the Colt in his right hand and the toothpick in his left as he went down the stairs. Halfway to the bottom he stopped.

The front door was open.

Fargo remembered it being closed. He descended the rest of the way and moved to the parlor. Clementine wasn't there. He glided to the kitchen but Clementine was there, either. The bolt had been thrown in the back door so he knew she hadn't gone out that way.

Every nerve raw, Fargo checked the pantry. Again, nothing. He retraced his steps to the parlor. She wasn't downstairs and she wasn't upstairs. Where else? he asked himself, and edged to the front door.

In the woods an owl hooted.

A sound came from the direction of the barn.

Slipping out, Fargo waited for his eyes to adjust. He wasn't taking any chances. He's seen what these crazies could do and he'd be damned if he'd end up like Dogood and Edna and Marshal Gruel.

Another sound from the vicinity of the barn brought him to the end of the porch.

Fargo crouched. It was important he spot her before she spotted him. His life might depend on it.

One of Dogood's horses whinnied.

Fargo was about to step off the porch when there was a hiss—from behind him.

# 28

Fargo whirled and brought up his Colt, or tried to. Clementine was on him before he was halfway around. She pounced on his back. Her nails raked his cheek and she screeched and thrust her mouth at his neck. Off-balance, he tripped off the porch and almost pitched onto his face. It saved him.

Clementine was thrown over his shoulders and landed at his feet.

Fargo took a step back but she grabbed his right boot and yanked. He fell hard, his shoulder blades catching the edge of the porch. His left arm went numb and he lost the toothpick.

With a fierce keen, Clementine scrambled toward him. He went to shoot her but she was incredibly quick. She seized his right wrist and clawed at his eyes. He jerked his face away and received deep scratches on his forehead. His hat flipped into the air.

Fargo sought to grab her hair but his left arm wouldn't work. Her mouth gaping wide, she bit at his cheek. He slammed his brow into her chin. It snapped her head back and elicited a hiss. He tried to heave her off but she had hold of the whangs on his shirt.

Clementine was drooling a flood. Her eyes blazed red with feral fury. She tried to sink her teeth into his throat and he rammed his arm up under her jaw. Thrashing and gnashing her teeth, she sought to sink them into him.

Fargo had to get her off. He couldn't hold her at bay indefinitely. And although he now knew her bites wouldn't infect him, she might sever an artery.

Tingling in his left arm let him know he had feeling in his fingers, and seizing her by the hair, he threw her down.

Clementine pushed into a crouch and bared her teeth.

Using his elbows, Fargo levered erect. He still had the Colt and he pointed it at her. He had her dead to rights but he remembered Belinda's plea and he hesitated. It cost him.

In a bound worthy of a mountain lion, Clementine slammed into his chest. He clipped her on the head and she fell but she was up again in a heartbeat.

Their fight had taken them to the middle of the porch. Fargo retreated to gain more space between them. Clementine came at him but stopped and glanced sharply at the front door.

Dreading what he would see, Fargo glanced over.

Belinda Jackson hadn't stayed upstairs. "Clementine," she said. "I can help you."

The madwoman snarled.

"You need to fight it," Belinda said slowly and calmly. "Use your willpower."

Clementine blinked and said, "Doc?" and flew at her. Belinda brought up her hands to protect herself. They collided, the impact knocking Belinda into the house with Clementine clinging to her like a cougar to a doe.

Fargo leaped to help and was brought up short by the screen door slamming in his face. He tore it open and darted in. The women were on the floor, Clementine hissing and snapping, Belinda doing all in her power to keep from having her throat torn out.

Cocking the Colt, Fargo jammed it against the back of Clementine's skull.

"No! Please!" Belinda pleaded while struggling. "Take her alive!"

Again Fargo hesitated. Again it proved costly.

Clementine's mouth dipped. Belinda's eyes went wide and she cried out.

Seizing Clementine by the shoulders, Fargo tore her off and shoved her away. He was too late.

A fist-sized chunk of flesh had been torn from Belinda's throat. Belinda's mouth moved but all that came out were mews of despair.

Screeching demonically, Clementine pushed to her hands and knees. Her mouth was red with Belinda's blood and pink bits of flesh were stuck in her teeth.

Fargo shot her in the throat. She hissed and reared to come at him and he shot her in the chest. She staggered, recovered, and sprang. He shot her smack between the eyes and she crumpled and lay in a quivering pile.

Belinda gurgled his name.

Sinking to a knee, Fargo clasped her hand. There was nothing he could do. Nothing anyone could do. She knew, and gave him a look of understanding and sympathy. "Damn you," he said.

Belinda tried to speak but all that came from her throat was a red mist. Her mouth parted, she arched her back, and was gone.

Fargo knelt there a while. Finally he stood and stepped over to Clementine and emptied the Colt into her face. When the hammer clicked on empty he went into the parlor and sat on the settee and reloaded. His hands shook a little but by the time the last cartridge was in the cylinder and he had twirled the Colt into his holster they were steady again. He went out and found the toothpick and slid it into his ankle sheath.

Taking a lamp, Fargo searched the barn. When he didn't find what he was looking for, he went to a shed near the back of the house. In it were the tools he needed: a shovel and a pick.

He dug for half an hour. No shallow grave for Belinda; he dug it good and deep and laid her out with care, crossing her arms over her chest and closing her eyes.

As for Clementine, he dragged her out by her heels and tossed her in the hog pen. He thought about doing the same with Charles T. Dogood.

Fargo needed a drink. He went to the kitchen and had to open every cupboard before he found a half-empty bottle of Mononga-hela. The burning as it went down felt good. He smacked his lips and shook himself and went out to the front porch and sat in the rocking chair.

The serenity of the night was like a punch to the gut. Fargo rocked and drank and rocked and drank and little by little the hor-ror drained out of him. He was feeling halfway restored when the creak and rattle of a wagon warned him he would soon have com-pany.

Fargo stayed in the rocking chair. He had a notion who it was and he hoped he was right. With Belinda gone he no longer had to hold back.

A firefly appeared, the light wobbling with the roll of the wheels. It was a buckboard and it came on fast to the orchard and up the lane. Orville and Mabel were in the seat. Orville stood and hauled on the reins to bring the team to a stop. He grabbed a rifle and jumped down.

"What about me?" Mabel said. "Aren't you goin' to help me off?"

"I thought you liked to do everythin' your own self," Orville said angrily. He slowed as he came to the Ovaro. "Look who's here."

"We'll put an end to him," Mabel said.

Orville strode past the van and up the steps and barreled into the house without a glance to either side.

"Consarn you," Mabel said. She hurried in after him, and she didn't glance at the rocking chair, either.

Fargo resumed his drinking and rocking.

"Are they in the kitchen?" Mabel hollered.

"No," Orville shouted from the back of the house.

"They must be upstairs, then. Come on."

Orville's heavy boots clomped and Mabel let out a strident, "Charlie!" They made a lot of noise going from room to room. Presently his boots thumped along the hall and the screen door slammed open and Orville strode out. He was holding the rifle by the stock with the barrel across his shoulder. "I don't understand it," he said. "The van is here and Charlie is up in that room dead as hell but where did Clementine get to?"

"She has to be here somewhere," Mabel said, emerging and standing next to him. She looked around and saw Fargo and froze. "Orville?" she said softly.

"What now?"

"Be real careful."

Orville glanced at her and then in the direction she was staring and he started to lower the rifle but must have thought better of it because he stopped and said, "You."

"Me," Fargo said, and took another swallow.

"We heard about what you did in town. Shot six of our kin dead."

"Was that all?"

Orville took a step to the right. "What happened to Charlie Dogood?"

"Someone mistook him for an apple." Fargo chuckled at his little joke.

"It's not funny, damn you," Orville said. "He's lyin' dead up there with his throat ripped out. Who did it?"

"Forget about him," Mabel said. "What I want to know is where our daughter is. Someone told us Charlie brought her out here along with that no-good doc."

"It's Dr. Jackson to you," Fargo said. "And whoever told you, told you right." He sipped and rolled the whiskey on his tongue. "Goes down smooth. Want some?"

Orville didn't know what to make of him. "Answer my wife. Where's Clementine? Who did that to Charlie? And where did that damn Belinda Jackson get to?"

"Which first?" Fargo said.

"Which what?"

"He means which question," Mabel said. "And the answer is we want to know about our daughter the most."

"All of this because of some water celery and mushrooms," Fargo said. "It's a hell of a world."

"What are you prattlin' about?" Mabel snapped.

"I'm answering your questions, bitch."

Orville took a step but Mabel grabbed his arm and shook her head.

"Let's hear what he has to say first."

Orville grunted.

"All that foaming at the mouth people have been doing?" Fargo said. "You have your good friend Dogood to thank. He mixed a poisonous plant with mushrooms and eighty-proof alcohol and opium. It's a wonder the first sip didn't kill them."

"You're makin' that up," Mabel said.

"I wish," Fargo said. He was almost done with the bottle. He swirled the whiskey and took a last swallow.

"Even if what you say is true," Mabel said, "it's not as if he did it on purpose, I bet."

"Who tore out his throat like that?" Orville asked. "Was it Dr. Jackson?"

"Dogood wasn't treating Belinda for anything," Fargo said. "It was Sawyer, Timmy, Abigail, and Clementine who drank the stuff."

They looked at one another.

"Your precious girl," Fargo said. "She had a cold so Dogood gave her a couple of bottles of his cure. It makes it fitting, I suppose, that she was the one who killed him."

"Where is she now?" Orville said.

Fargo set the bottle on the porch and stood. "I fed her to the hogs."

"You did what now?" Mabel said.

"If you hurry over, there might be some of her left."

Orville glanced toward the hog pen and his features hardened. With a loud oath he swung his rifle level.

Fargo drew and shot him in the chest, three swift shots, one after the other.

"Orville!" Mabel cried, and tried to catch him but he was much too heavy and crashed to the porch, his rifle clattering.

Bending, she cradled his head. "Orville, speak to me. Tell me you ain't dead."

"Dead as hell," Fargo said. He walked around her to the steps.

"I hate you," Mabel said. "I hate you more than anything. I should kill you my own self."

"Did I mention that Dogood was poking your daughter? He seduced her years ago and she's been his secret lover ever since."

"You're lying!"

Fargo remembered Mabel tarring Belinda, remembered her hitting Belinda, remembered her doing all she could to make Belinda's life miserable. "How does it feel to be the mother of a slut?"

Mabel threw back her head and screeched. She saw her husband's rifle and snatched it up. "I'm goin' to kill you, you son of a bitch."

"No," Fargo said, "you're not." He shot her in the head, puffed on the smoke that rose from the end of the barrel, and walked to the Ovaro. Shoving the Colt into his holster, he forked leather. "Good riddance," he said to the bodies on the porch.

A flick of the reins and a tap of his spurs and he rode off into the dark Ozark night.

# LOOKING FORWARD!
## The following is the opening section of the next novel in the exciting *Trailsman* series from Signet:

## TRAILSMAN #364
## ROCKY MOUNTAIN RUCKUS

*Montana (Northern Nebraska Territory), 1860—
where Death takes the pleasing form of three
beautiful sisters with a secret.*

"Fargo, I got a God fear that somebody is following us," said Captain Jasper Dundee.

Skye Fargo, riding out ahead on the rock-strewn mountain trail, nodded. He was a tall man clad in buckskins, wide in the shoulders and narrow in the hips. "Been following us for the better part of two hours, I'd reckon."

Dundee, a weathered campaign veteran of the U.S. Cavalry's Department of Dakota, slewed around in the saddle to study their back trail. "Redskins, you think?"

Fargo shook his head. "You know how it is with the red aborigines, Jasp. When they take a notion to follow you, you won't know it until you hear the war whoop. No, these are white men."

"That rings right to me, Trailsman. And seeing's how white men are scarce as hen's teeth this high up, it's a good chance these slinking coyotes are Dub Kreeger and his gang of deserters. Might even have their sights notched on us right now."

Fargo whipped the dust from his hat and twisted around to grin at the officer. "Could be. Let's hope Army marksmanship training is as piss-poor as I believe it is."

Fargo faced front again, his eyes crimped to slits in the brilliant, spun-gold sunshine of a summer day in the Rocky Mountains. Some of the fringes on his faded buckskins were crusted with old blood. His crop-bearded face was half in shadow under the broad brim of a white plainsman's hat.

The breathtaking view out ahead of them was familiar to Fargo, but he always gazed upon it as if seeing it for the first time. Many back in the States still believed the Rocky Mountains were a single wall rather than a series of parallel ranges. He could see them clearly now like ascending curtain folds, with the cloud-nestled spires of the imposing Bitterroot Range forming the final great barrier to human exploration.

"Think we'll ever tame 'em?" Dundee called out behind him. "These mountains, I mean."

Fargo mulled that one. Two decades earlier Hudson's Bay Company men had swarmed this region until driven out by Nathaniel Wyeth's Rocky Mountain Fur Company. But the London dandies no longer craved beaver hats, and now the region was mostly populated by Indians, silver and gold miners, soldiers, and a few hearty independent trappers. Fargo considered this land bordering the rugged Canadian Rockies one of the most pristine and spectacular places in the West—but also in grave danger of being overrun by "cussed syphillization."

"Tame them, no," he finally replied. "Leastways I hope not. But unless the New York land hunters and the rest of them nickel-chasing fools back east are reined in, these mountains will be blasted into slag heaps by the miners and railroad barons."

"Spoken like a true bunch-quitter," Dundee said.

Something glinted from the slope above the pass.

"See that?" Dundee called forward.

Fargo nodded. "That wasn't quartz or mica, not this far up. Hell, our horses are blowing hard even at a walk. Knock your riding thong off, Jasp, and break out your carbine—we might have a set-to coming."

"Suits me right down to the ground. I'd admire to ventilate Dub Kreeger's skull. I knew that crooked bastard back at Fort Robinson. Just another scheming snowbird—joined the army in fall to get out of the cold, then lit out at the first spring thaw. Only, he liberated three hundred dollars from the Widows and Orphans Fund before he and his greasy bootlicks left."

"I heard he got himself arrested in the Black Hills?"

"That's the straight," Dundee confirmed. "All four of 'em were in the stockade. They shoulda danced on air long ago. But they killed two guards and pulled a bust out. Made off with two cases of ammo, too. Lately they've taken to this high country and raiding on the new Overland route between South Pass and the Oregon Territory."

Dundee paused to survey the slopes around them. "Damn fool idea, Fargo, this new Overland route."

"Sure it is. But it was also a damn fool idea for the army to build the road that made it possible. All it did was stir up the featherheads."

"That's exactly what I told Colonel Halfpenny. There's no civilian law up here and damn few soldiers. Now there's three way-station men murdered, two Overland teamsters missing, a payroll missing, and God knows what happened to the three widows. And to cap the climax, Flathead Indian attacks have closed off the route and marooned Robert's Station."

"Oh, there's law up here," Fargo gainsaid. "Gun law. But I'm with you on all the rest. And sending one soldier into these mountains is dicey enough, if you take my drift."

Dundee took it, all right. He and Fargo had been sent out of Fort Seeley to investigate the apparent heist of an army payroll as well as the fate of missing civilians. Seeley was a small garrison meant to protect prospectors in the Bitterroot Range. But a troop movement this high into the mountains could ignite a full-blown Indian war, especially with the Flathead tribe whose clan circles dotted this region.

Fargo's Ovaro flicked his ears several times. Since there were no flies at this altitude, Fargo read it as a warning the stallion was picking up sounds—sounds that didn't naturally belong to the area.

"Trouble's on the spit," he told Dundee. "But since they're up above us, there's no point in holing up. We'd be fish in a barrel. Our smartest play is to keep them back out of range until we hit the new federal road, then outrun 'em. Break out your spyglasses and glom that slope good."

"If it's the Kreeger bunch," Dundee opined as he pulled out his brass field glasses, "they'll likely have their stolen army Spencers. It's a good weapon at the short and middle distances, but that short barrel makes it unreliable over three hundred yards."

Several minutes passed in silence, the only sounds the hoof clops of their mounts and the occasional moaning of wind funneling through the pass. But Fargo felt the presence of imminent danger, as real as the man beside him.

"You know anything about these three widows?" Fargo asked.

Dundee chuckled. "I wondered when you'd get around to them, Lothario. No, I don't know much. But all three are sisters, and my hand to God, they were married to three brothers."

"Ever meet these brothers?"

"Nope. According to our records, they were named Stanton— Cort, Lemuel, and Addison Stanton. Hardworking and honest according to Overland."

"How do you know for sure they were killed?"

"An express rider found the bodies, all shot in the head. Sounds like the payroll coach showed up at the station minus the driver and messenger guard. These three fellows went out to see if they could find the missing men."

Fargo nodded. "Well, last I heard the Flathead tribe has very few barking irons. Besides, they like to take prisoners alive and bring them back to the village for torture. If a prisoner acts tough and stands up to it good, they'll generally let him go."

"Mighty white of 'em," Dundee said sarcastically.

"More than you'll get from an Apache or Comanche, soldier blue. So what about the strongbox?"

"Yeah, what about it? I agree with you that white men likely killed those teamsters, and that almost surely means Dub Kreeger and his two-legged roaches. I s'pose they got it."

"I don't," Fargo said flatly. "Not if that's the Kreeger gang watching us right now."

Dundee, still watching through his glasses, let that remark sink in for a minute. "Yeah, all right, you've got a good point and I'm caught upon it. If that pack of yellow curs laid their paws on twenty-eight thousand dollars, why in blue blazes would they still be in this area, right? Sure as cats fighting they'd be on their way to San Francisco or Santa Fe."

Fargo nodded. "So either they didn't get it or that's not them getting set to perforate our livers."

"Fargo, you've got a poetical way of speaking," Dundee said sarcastically.

Again the Ovaro pricked his ears, but this time Fargo wasn't so sure it was a danger sign—his own frontier-honed ears picked up faint sounds from the right side of the trail. Sounds remarkably like feminine laughter.

"Jasp," he called out, "light down and hobble your mount. Bring your spyglasses, too."

"Trouble?"

"Most likely—sounds like females."

Both men swung down, tied their horses foreleg to rear with rawhide strips, then wormed their way through the boulders massed along the trail. A minute later they emerged onto a large traprock shelf overlooking a small valley with a white-water stream churning through it.

Dundee stared, jaw slacked in astonishment, then brought his field glasses up for a better look. Fargo followed suit.

"Son of a splayfooted bitch," Dundee said in a reverent whisper. "Are you seeing the same thing I am, Fargo?"

"Yeah. We can't both be dreaming."

Below, in the center of the verdant valley, the noisy stream crashed over a rock lip, forming a small waterfall and a natural pool. Three young women, shapely, pretty, and naked as jaybirds, frolicked in the pool.

Fargo said, "There's our three widows, I'd wager. Don't appear to be mourning, either."

"Well, keep up the strut! Two gorgeous brunettes and a blonde who looks like the youngest," Dundee said. "The only place I've seen tits like that is on those French playing cards."

"These ain't psalm singers neither," Fargo said, glancing at the formidable cache of weapons at the edge of the pool. "These three nymphs are loaded for bear."

"A woman should be well-heeled up in these mountains, Trails-man."

"Actually, a woman shouldn't be up here at all."

However, Fargo's words lacked all conviction as he watched one of the brunettes bend over to scrub her legs.

"Look at that, won'tcha?" Dundee said in a voice gone raspy with lust. "That sweet, firm ass baying at the moon. And look! The blonde is sudsing her tits! Jesus, Fargo, maybe we'll roll a seven, huh? They got no men now."

"We're ordered to bring them down out of the mountains, Jasp, not to bed them."

Still staring through his glasses, Captain Dundee made a fart-ing noise with his lips. "You sanctimonious hypocrite! Christ, every morning you have to comb the pussy hair out of your teeth. You telling me you don't plan to tap into that stuff?"

Fargo grinned. "I'm a man likes a challenge, so I aim to hop on all three of 'em. Then I'll trim each one separately."

Dundee laughed. "I'm ugly and going bald, so I'll settle for just one. Maybe—"

Dundee never got his next word out. Fargo heard a sickening sound like a hammer hitting a watermelon followed a fractional second later by the reverberating crack of a cavalry carbine. The back of Dundee's head exploded in a scarlet blossom, and the offi-cer folded to the ground like an empty sack.